9781434428677

THE VOLGA BOATMAN

A Cecil B. De Mille Production. *The Volga Boatman*
WITH THE HANDSOME IMAGE OF FEODOR IN HER HEART,
MARIUSHA SCORNS THE POOR BLACKSMITH'S DEVOTION.

THE VOLGA BOATMAN

BY
KONRAD BERCOVICI

ILLUSTRATED WITH SCENES
FROM THE PHOTOPLAY
Personally Directed by
CECIL B. DE MILLE

NEW YORK
GROSSET & DUNLAP
PUBLISHERS

Made in the United States of America

COPYRIGHT, 1926, BY
GROSSET & DUNLAP

To
CECIL B. DE MILLE
WHO CALLED ME THREE THOUSAND
MILES TO LISTEN TO THIS
STORY

THE VOLGA BOATMAN

THE VOLGA BOATMAN

CHAPTER I

THIS is the kind of story that has neither a beginning nor an end. Most stories begin somewhere, and you stop because you don't know what happened further. This is more of a wound than a story. And you know how wounds are. It may hurt a little more and make a deeper hole in the flesh, but it is far better to cut deeper, more so than necessary, in order to make sure that what remains of the flesh is sound and untainted. The largest clean wound heals much faster than a small one that has not been properly cleansed. So you will forgive me if I begin the story a little further back than seemingly necessary.

Let me tell you first of Kniaz Nikita. As a man of about forty, he had come down to live in his castle near Saratov on the Volga River, from abroad, where he had passed his early youth while his father, the old kniaz, had been administering the immense property of the Nikitas. Ivan Ivanoff and another man were pulling a boat down the Volga from Nijni Novgorod. Do you know how boats are navigated down on that river? Two men are harnessed to a long rope that crosses from over the left shoulder and under the right, with the other end of the rope fastened to a ring in the side of the boat. Then the boat is pulled along the shore while it is being guided by a long pole by one of the men on the prow.

While the weather was warm they pulled the boat walking in bare feet, trousers rolled up to the knees and the shirt open at the neck. Stopping at nightfall, they made campfires, very much like gypsies, around which they ate their food, falling asleep on the warm ground, to rise in the morning with the dawn, and continue up or down the river as luck would have it. There was always an up-river trip, for they had to bring back the boat to the starting point.

When the weather was not so clement as to permit the boatmen to sleep on the ground they would sleep on board boat after anchoring it safely. Frequently when they happened to pass alongside one of the villages one of them would pass the night at the inn alongside the shores. And those were gay nights, with gypsies and women and much drinking. At the end of a round trip they were lucky if there remained money to buy a meal and a bed for the night. Such is the Volga boatman's life.

Sometimes the trip down the river to Astrakhan, where the Volga empties itself into the Caspian Sea, lasted several months, and they had to stay there quite a while before the boat was unloaded of the lumber or the grain it carried. But those were gay days, most of them. For the peasants would always sit around the boatmen and offer them drink at the inns whenever they passed by, to listen to the tales brought from along the river, tales that filtered down from all parts of the world, from India and from China, from Japan and from all other ends of the world. And there were things the boatmen always carried with them, things bought here and there for the young girls and young widows who were waiting for them.

Kniaz Nikita had neither beard nor mustache. Unlike his father, who had worn Russian clothes about his place, this young kniaz still wore the clothes he had brought with him from Paris or elsewhere. Because of that the people around him did not like him as well as they had liked the father, nor did they serve him as well.

True, the old kniaz occasionally used his whip on the backs of the men. But he was one of them. He would drink vodka together with them on occasions.

His drunkenness had two forms. He would either get so angry that he would lash out with his whip on all the men about him, running about his estate with his whip in hand like a savage, or he would be so gay he would insist on dancing with all the muzhiks of the village, and finish up by having his arms about them and calling them brothers; emptying his pockets to them of all the paper roubles he carried with him, and even giving them the jewelry from his fingers. And there was many a youngster in the village, the son of a servant or administrator, who resembled him much more than did his own son, Kniaz Nikita, who took his place at the head of the kniazly palace at the death of the old man.

Kniaz Nikita at forty brought with himself a wife from somewhere in the west, as his father had brought one from Germany. All the kniazes brought for themselves wives from other parts of the world. The old kniaz himself was the son of such a mother. But none of them had come back as un-Russian as Vladimir Gregorevitch Nikita. None of them had such a sad and worn face.

It was a long time after he had ruled his house and his village before anybody had heard him say a word, either good or bad. He was too superior to talk to any one. He looked like a lion that had not resigned himself to his cage.

But life would not have it so. After the peasants round him had not seen him for a few weeks the news spread round the huts of the neighborhood that the kniaz had grown a mustache. A little later it was observed that he was growing a beard. Before the end of the second year he had grown a full flowing red beard, which with his long hair and mustache made him look more like his father; and then people began to like him a little better.

And being more friendly to them, they talked to him. And he answered in kindly tones and said kind words to all of them in their own language. And as he had to stay on his property most of the year, people said because it was so willed by his father, after he got tired of all the books and of listening to the piano playing of his German wife, he began to do as his father had done. The day Ivan passed by, harnessed to a boat that carried lumber, Kniaz Nikita was celebrating together with the peasants in the enclosure of his castle the harvest festival. He had put on his father's own Russian costume, and thus had taken on a good many of his father's habits. That very morning he had whipped several gypsies with his own hands for no reason at all. Repenting a little afterwards, he had sent several men on horseback to find the gypsies who had run away, and had them brought back more dead than alive, for they were afraid that the kniaz was going to whip them to death. But he hugged them and kissed them in the presence of all the people, and amused himself for a half hour filling their violins through the two holes under the bridge with gold pieces of which he had his pockets full. And while they were playing he was still keeping his arms about them, kissing them and calling them little brothers, to the horror of the kniazina, his wife, who was standing a little aside with two of her chambermaids, because he had ordered her to be about. If she refused he threatened to whip her and her whole Frentresca crew. He was like that.

The crust of polish gone he was a Russian kniaz.

Ivan's companion, who harnessed together with him had pulled the boat down to Saratov from Jaroslav, was called Feodor. Kazan was his home. He was a man of about thirty. Ivan had met him years before one winter at Nijni Novgorod, at one of the inns. He was drunk, and talking, standing on a table, to the peasants who happened to be there. And what he said at that time, the first time Ivan had laid his eyes on him, would have been enough to hang him if anybody had cared to denounce him. The peasants stood about his table, half drunk themselves, leaning on knotted sticks and laughing, though they only half understood what he said. They were amused and continually filled his glass with vodka from the bottles, that he might drink and tell more. And Feodor, hatless, coatless, with a stout rope instead of a belt to hold up his trousers, with his long arms waving in the air, was telling them all about the time to come when everybody would be a kniaz and every one would have his fill of everything desired, when he and the others would no longer have to go to the inn to drink themselves to forgetfulness, because there would not be anything unpleasant to forget. Even while drinking he was cursing drink as the source of all evil in Russia, as the source of all evil in the world. And the drunken peasants laughed and gave him more drink; that he amuse them with his talk and drunken curses.

The peasants were beginning to be moved by something they did not understand when Feodor, leaning over them, kept shouting:

"Don't you see? Don't you see, you drunken louts? The Czar, his satellites and the landowners are sucking you dry of your blood."

As his shirt was open at the chest Ivan could see from the thick red welt that crossed it from left to right that he was a boatman. The rope had left its mark. Ivan's heart warmed to Feodor. He had money to spend. It was winter; the end of winter. Another month or two and the Volga would again be open for boating. Ivan had not liked his companion in harness of the former year, and had decided to look for another one for the coming season. He liked Feodor. It seemed to him that it would be a great joy to have him as a steady companion. Any man who could talk as he did, could cry as he did, would also be gay and merry on occasions. The other man

THE VOLGA BOATMAN

he had been with had been a sad-eyed, sad-voiced fellow who would take everything out of Ivan's pockets when he was asleep, drunk, somewhere, and then pretend he did not know anything about it.

When he had quietened and clambered down from the table Ivan walked up to him.

"Tavarish," he said, "I can see from the mark of the rope that you are a boatman."

Instantly in his hoarse voice he began to sing the boatman song. Before the hour was over they were blood brothers.

However, there was one thing about him that made Ivan uneasy. He had queer ways of talking and snapping his finger in the air when contradicted. He had heard in his travel somewhere, words of a better world, words of a world where everybody could be as happy as everybody else, with no hunger and no thirst, and no coatless backs when the snows were falling, no half naked children smothering under feather beds through the winter months, and fed bread of which only half was flour and the other a mixture of the bark of trees and powdered leaves.

He was right in all he said. The Czar's Russia was a terrible place to live in, but Ivan was afraid to hear him talk so wildly.

Ivan took up quarters at the inn for the winter, and meanwhile kept close watch on Feodor. What a strange man he was! When he had sobered up the following morning he shaved himself and cleaned himself as if he were a school teacher. He stood in front of a little mirror and cut his hair short, not as the peasants wore it hanging over the shoulders; and cut his beard and his mustache, and washed himself and rubbed himself and scrubbed himself; more finicky than a town girl about his appearance. And yet he had sold his coat, sold his fur cap, sold his boots and sold his suspenders that he had bought in the market of Kazan the previous fall, sold all to the innkeeper for the bottles of vodka that he had drunk the previous day.

Ivan had some roubles in his pocket, and loaned them to Feodor. And now, sobered up as he was, it was he who was speaking against drunkards, he who was speaking against drunkenness, and was telling Ivan that in the world of happy people he was dreaming that the first thing they would do would be to abolish drink and thereby drunkenness, for it was one of the causes of the unhappiness of the world. And he knew so many things about it. He pointed out the many diseases that came as a consequence of drunkenness.

That night instead of going to the inn Feodor pulled out several little paper-covered booklets from the bottom of his trunk. And he began to read to Ivan of the happier world, from one of these little booklets which were distributed all over Russia. They used to be left in the school benches by some invisible hand for the children to carry home after reading them on the way. Those little booklets used to be found at the doors of churches and at the tables at inns and sleeping places, little booklets that had been given me everywhere along the way by men who seemed to have their pockets full of nothing else.

While Ivan and Feodor were in a little room over the inn, lying down on the straw mattress, many of the peasants would come knocking at the door, begging that Feodor should come down and talk to them. They wanted to hear him talk. They wanted him to come down and drink with them. And they were angry when he refused, and accused Ivan of having come to spoil their fun with their best friend.

And how right Feodor was about it! Even as he had been reading to Ivan from another book in which all was explained about the amount of land a man should have in order to make a living, even while he read from that book how little money was used to give the people of Russia an education, while in other countries fifty and sixty times as much was used for the same purpose, even while he was reading of all that, a fight broke out among the peasants below them at the inn over some trifle or other, and when that fight was over there were several men crippled for life if not at the point of death. And the ones who had crippled them were weeping and tearing their hair and getting more drunk because they were suffering so terribly from remorse.

He did not stay sober, Feodor, all the time. He had traveled and seen many things. And he would occasionally forget his own teachings and drink, and when Ivan reproached him he would merely refer to the same writings and say:

"Yes, but am I not one of the very people they speak about in the books? We get drunk because there is not any other happiness for us. We get drunk because we are sad and worried."

He always said "we" when he did something he himself did not approve of. He excused himself by claiming to be one of the millions of Russians, no better and no worse than the rest.

He would lean on Ivan's shoulder and weep and cry, and defend his own drunkenness with as much eloquence as he spoke against it. And the whole thing would wind up by Ivan getting as drunk as Feodor, as if he wanted to confirm by his own condition the truth of Feodor's words.

When Feodor was drunk, he spoke about his wife and children, to whom he intended to return as soon as he had sobered up. Yet he forgot them when he was sober. When Ivan reproached him for his forgetfulness one day, he said that he had learned it was much better for a man like him to be unshackled, free. Children belonged to the world and not to a father and mother. That the new world, the new order of things, was soon to be inaugurated. Then it would be much better for children to feel that they belonged to the state, to the government, that the state was the father, instead of one man directing their destinies according to his own lights.

Soldiering, the Japanese war, had given Feodor a taste of the road, and Ivan knew that when one had been pulling boats along the

Volga one could never settle down anywhere and live the life of a peasant. One became very much as gypsies, even more so, because one did not have his family about him wandering from one place to the other. One could never again settle down on a narrow strip of land to the yoke of a family and work in the fields after one had slept near a campfire and been master of his own time at night, and of the days at the inns. Freedom is like drink, whoever has tasted it wants it again, wants it to the last drop in the pitcher. The Volga boatmen had only one yoke on their shoulders. When they threw that off they were free. The peasants were hobbled by unseen chains on which dragged heavy balls that clattered on the uneven ground. Wife, children, beasts, poverty, the landlord, the government, rain, drought, locusts, vermin. The Volga boatmen were free of all that. They had only one stout rope that tied them to the boat. Otherwise they were free.

CHAPTER II

THEN the war came. Feodor was taken and then Ivan was taken, and because they had been on boats they were put on board ships, and sent away to patrol the Caspian Sea from imaginary enemies which they never saw and never heard of, although they were shooting their cannons from time to time. They roved about from Astrakhan to Balkan and from Gouriev to Graspovodka.

They really did not know what was happening at home during all these years in which they were kept in absolute idleness, cruising on the Caspian Sea. And if one of the boats was occasionally blown up in the air, it was not by an enemy mine, but from one of the Russian's own mines. Russia was killing her own men instead of waiting for the enemy to do it. Russia was sinking her own ships.

At one of the landings Ivan caught sight of Feodor, and they passed a few merry hours together talking of this and that. He had changed considerably, Feodor. He had obtained a rank in the navy and was keeping himself clean and spotless, always shaved, always neat. He had become a little quieter than he had been before, knew more things and talked more intelligently about what he talked of before. When Ivan used to ask him in former days how the great day of the new humanity was to be ushered in, he never knew any definite way. It was always some power outside him over which he had no control, which he did not know, but which was to do it. But now he seemed to know definitely. It was all clear to him. The people had to be educated into knowing. He no longer talked loud in everybody's hearing about his plans. It was important, he said, that those who knew what he knew should be free, not in the jails, and gain the respect and the love of the people they associated with. And he had that, Feodor. The sailors loved him. He had organized the sailors of his boat into a singing choir. He had a beautiful voice and knew so many folk songs and river songs that it was a pleasant way to while away hours of idleness singing them. Ivan heard him direct his choir on board his boat, at another time, a year later, when they met in Petrovsk, where the boats had gone for repairs.

Meanwhile Feodor had gained another braid on his sleeve. He had risen higher in

THE VOLGA BOATMAN 17

rank. And still the sailor-soldiers under him loved him and respected him.

Ivan had not advanced in rank. Feodor reproached him his untidiness and occasional drunkenness. There is no more sedentary and lonesome occupation than that of a sailor. Tempest and storm are welcomed because they break the monotony of the sameness of the sky and the sea. How different along the Volga, where everything changed from day to day.

But all things came to an end, and that too came to an end. Suddenly the news came one day that the end of the war was soon to come. It did not matter who was the winner. The important thing was the war was soon to come to an end. The feeling of the sailors and the people was that it was well that the war had come to an end. They would not have suffered less if the Czar had won the war, and they could not suffer more if the Czar was the loser. There was no question among the people as to who won. The only thing was that the war had come to an end. And right with that came the news about the Czar's forced abdication, and then the revolution, and then the Kerensky government that followed it. And Russia was to join the Allies again and fight. She had been betrayed by the Czar, the Czarina, Rasputin and the others. Now they were to fight again and this time they had to win because they had no more Czar. Russia was a republic. Russia was their Russia.

And then came the news that sailors had seized ships, chained their commanders and taken charge of the vessels themselves. Ivan's crew did not seize their ship. They were debarked at Derbent, in Lower Caucas. All things had changed again. They were not to war any more. Ivan was only too glad to get rid of the whole thing and return to his own village for a spell. In the many years he had never thought of it. Only when he was so far away, in the war, he was wondering what was happening to his old mother and what was happening to his other brothers. Several of them, at least two of them, had probably been taken into the war, and Ivan wondered how they had come out.

With a little bundle of things on his shoulders he set out on foot for his village, after saying good-by to his comrades. Along the way the villages were seething with all kinds of new plans and new rumors. Everybody seemed to have abandoned work for talk.

People assembled in front of churches and on corners of roads and in front of houses and inns and talked and talked incessantly, each one saying what he wished Russia to be from then on, what he hoped Russia would become from then on. A spider web of plans hung over Russia, as if people could live on plans!

And Ivan wanted to see his people. He wondered about them and worried about them. And the next other thing he wanted to see Feodor. He wanted to talk to him. He wanted to hear from him what had already happened.

On the fourteenth day Ivan reached home. It was a small village of about two hundred inhabitants on the shore of the river Kouma, twenty versts from Stavropol. There never had been great plenty in the fields. But there was plenty of fish, and so the people there had always been happier and better fed than the people in most parts of Russia. And because they could prepare enough dry fish for the winter, and had staples and hay, the cows had food and gave them plenty of milk. Their cows were fed on fish the whole winter long.

Ivan had not seen his mother in eight years. The youngest child, Sonia, his sister, was now eighteen years old. Vania had not come back from the war. He had not been heard of from the first day he had left. Nikolai, the second brother, returned and arrived home minus his left arm and left leg the day after Ivan came home. He was five years younger than Ivan, but he looked an old man. He had hobbled home on his crutches, begging his way through, although in military uniform, for the last four weeks. And now all he wanted was to eat and sleep. Ivan tried to talk to him. He wanted to know in what battles he had been. The poor cripple looked blankly, asked for more food and leaned back to sleep. He had become an idiot.

The two hundred inhabitants of the village had formed themselves in forty different committees now and had taken charge of everything within the village. Instead of one Czar in St. Petersburg there were forty little Czars right at home. Each one knowing how things should be done differently, and how things had to be done. Although they called one another "tavarishe" they were just as many little autocratic Czars. Each one asked Ivan whether he was for the old or for the new, and no one could have told what the new was. And so Ivan wanted even more to see Feodor. He wanted to see Feodor and wanted

THE VOLGA BOATMAN 21

to go back to the Volga. His shoulders longed for the rope around them. His body just itched to take again the large steps, with the feet well planted in the soil, pulling the boat, singing the boatman song to the rhythmic splash of the waves of the river. What cared he for the old or for the new! They were both stupid!

So one morning Ivan left home and brothers and started out towards Astrakhan.

He took up on the road with a gypsy band of musicians. They were thoroughly scared by the changes that had taken place. They had been playing in the homes of the rich and at the inns where the wealthy people assembled. Even during the war they had been doing that. When the Russians were beaten the rich men wanted drink and music to drown their sadness. When they had been victorious they sang and drank to celebrate. Gypsies were always in demand.

But now everything was topsy-turvy. No one wanted to hear their songs, no one wanted to hear them play. They were useless. There was no trading in horses or cows. They were like birds in a treeless, grassless waste.

Everything we have done or do appears to us in a different light at different times. We have one manner of thinking before we do a certain thing, one manner of thinking while we are doing it, and a different manner of thinking afterwards. And if we had to tell every time how we think we would never tell the truth. We would probably tell at the time we want to do a thing in the same manner as if we were to tell it long after we had done it.

There was a girl in Mischa's camp. She could not have been more than fifteen when Ivan first saw her; and he was already thirty. And he lusted for her. It is the real word. He lusted for her the moment he saw her. When he attached himself to the gypsies' camp he talked to them soothingly, trying to quieten their fears of what was to befall them in the near future. He used many of Feodor's phrases about the great brotherhood of man that was to come, in which even the gypsies would be equal to all other men and treated as such. Day to come! The day was already here. They were equals.

And so these poor, harassed, frightened people begged Ivan to stay with them, feeding him on the way and questioning him that he should tell them more about it so that they should feel more secure. He could call the people who addressed them "tavarish" and

THE VOLGA BOATMAN

tell them that these were his friends. It seemed to them that Ivan belonged to a brotherhood from which they were still excluded.

He remained with them, but it was not to allay their fears that he did so, but because he lusted for Mariusha. He had seen her half bare bosom and her bare legs; and because he had been without a woman for a long time she appeared to be the most beautiful woman he had ever seen. His limbs ached with the passion to touch hers. Perhaps the gypsies knew that Mariusha was one of the reasons he was staying with them. There were no other young women in that caravan, and except a few young boys there were no young men, for they had all been taken in the war and their bones were probably rotting at the bottom of the Masurian marshes.

He spread his net carefully. It was not that Ivan desired to marry her or have her with him. Though in the turmoil in which the brotherhood of man was to be ushered in, people spoke about abandoning all forms of marriage completely, he still thought of marriage in the old fashion. True, Feodor had run away from his wife, but he considered himself a married man. Ivan did not want to saddle himself with a gypsy woman as a wife.

He thought that if he ever married it was to be a peasant woman, his own kind.

It was very difficult to be near Mariusha except occasionally, and then for only a few brief moments. There were only four wagons in the caravan, dragged by old, starved horses. In two of the wagons were the women and in the others the men. They moved only very slowly because the horses were tired and starved. Ivan frequently wondered from where the food came to nourish them all. From somewhere in the wagons, from secret holds in them, a little food appeared from time to time after much wailing and crying. They got a little corn meal at one place for shoeing a horse, for these gypsies knew everything, and a bottle of brandy at another place for playing the new anthem which nobody seemed to know. At another place they were invited to a wedding which was held quite in the usual manner; for the priest of that village had kept his people in the old ways. He had even wanted the gypsies to play the Czar's anthem.

And while the men were playing Ivan stole away to the wagon of the women. They had all gone away, probably foraging for food for the following day while the people were busy dancing and singing. Mariusha was there. She seemed quite willing.

THE VOLGA BOATMAN

"But will you stay with us afterwards?" she asked, looking Ivan in the eyes when he put his arms about her.

He was taken aback, for he did not know whether she wanted him to stay with them because she desired and loved him, or because she wanted him to assure the security of her people.

Yet he said, "Always. Always." Men say such things.

While they held one another tightly they heard the music play at the wedding, and Mariusha grinned prettily and said:

"You see they are playing for our wedding."

And her limbs burned with passion. Her lips were so hot they seared Ivan's when they kissed. She made one wild with passion. Ivan would have welcomed death in her arms, with his arms about her and his head on her bosom. And her body yielded to his.

What had seemed to be very difficult at first began to be much easier afterwards, for Mariusha was now helping him to be alone with her. And in this she was much abler than he had been. All the passion Ivan could have anticipated in her was there, and much more of it. She seemed to be as anxious to be in his arms as he was to be in hers. And it seemed to him that the horses had suddenly taken on new life and that the wheels were running much faster. His tongue became untied. He remembered of a sudden long speeches of Feodor, and no longer being afraid to utter them, Ivan too began to speak at the corners of the crossroads and in front of churches and schools, and began to be part of all the agitation and movement and change that was taking place. And with Mariusha standing aside as an admirer he was fired to great eloquence. He talked. He preached to people.

Yet although Ivan desired Mariusha so much he already began to devise plans how to get rid of her when the time should come. He could see himself going from place to place talking to the people and being their idol, even as he imagined Feodor was at that time. And yet how the gypsy girl's charm held him. How he dreaded the moment when he should have to leave her! He had told the gypsies, when he had joined them, that he was going to leave them at Kazan. And if he did not leave them at Kazan he told them that he was sure to leave them at Nijni Novgorod. When they approached Kazan, Ivan did not dare speak of it to Mariusha.

CHAPTER III

THEY reached Kazan one morning. It was the day in which it was rumored the Germans had closed peace at Brest-Litovsk. A new government had come to be, to replace the Kerensky government, with which everybody already seemed to be dissatisfied because it had not fulfilled all the promises it had given, and the expectations which had been in people's minds, even those that had not been raised in them by the new government. And again there were the forty little Czars; the forty new little Czars in every village to replace forty old ones whose reins had been taken from them. And again there were things one was allowed to say and other things one was not. People seemed to think that they could raise wheat and corn in the fields by talking about it, that they could make schools by talking about them. And the women seemed to talk even more than the men. Suddenly they discovered that the churches were at the bottom of all ills. And all was topsy turvy, turmoil. Ivan longed for the river. He longed to hear the boatman song sung along the Volga. And he longed to see Feodor and talk it over with him. And there was Mariusha from whom he could not separate, did not know how to separate, and did not always want to separate. He was even a bit afraid of her. He had seen an ugly gleam in her eyes. During a passionate embrace she had told Ivan:

"If you ever leave me I shall kill you no matter when or where. Even if I come upon you twenty years later."

And, lo, at Kazan Ivan met Feodor in the street. But what a different Feodor from the one he had last seen. He too had come back to see his people after the war. And of all the people who talked in his village he talked less, though he knew more. After they had embraced and hugged one another, Ivan asked him:

"Surely, Feodor, you have been at the head of the movement that took the ships from the hands of their commanders?"

"No, I was not," Feodor said. "I argued against it, and because I was against it and was a petty officer they bound me and gagged me, and treated me as if I were their worst enemy. I was treated as a counter-revolutionist. I. I."

"How that?" Ivan asked.

Feodor shrugged his shoulders.

"They are so stupid! So stupid!"

"But surely you have helped change Russia?" I asked.

"I have not," he answered. "For I suddenly got scared of the change when I saw how it was being handled by those who were changed. And so I came home. I wanted to be near my people. I have a wife here," he told Ivan, "and children. We are ten versts from Kazan."

The whole caravan went to his village the same day. He disappointed Ivan. He thought Feodor was cowardly, that he had only been talking about things he did not believe in. When the things he had talked about had come he was the first one scared—the first one who tried to deny all that he had said.

And yet Ivan loved Feodor and having found him could not separate easily from him. He was still in many respects the old Feodor whom Ivan liked, and with whom he could talk and whom he could understand.

To make the matter worse now Mariusha and her people were continually nagging Ivan and asking him to continue with them on the way. They had pitched their tents a stone's throw from Feodor's home. Ivan had thought of Mariusha as a little chit of a girl at first, from whom he was to take pleasure through cajolery or by force. But he was mistaken. It was a different Mariusha than the one he had taken in his arms a few weeks before. She seemed to have grown ten years in that many days. It was Ivan now who felt trapped, instead of feeling guilty of having trapped her.

He put her people off from day to day. And when she insisted one day more than at the other times he cried out:

"I never told you that I was going to stay with you for ever and ever. I am not a gypsy. I told you I was going to Kazan."

And he told her something about the new order of things whereby a man was not tied on eternally to a woman. He was a man of the new order of things.

But to this Mariusha answered, and her breath was like fire from the nostrils of a wild beast.

"I have never asked about any laws. I am a gypsy. We have never followed any of your laws. We have our own laws. Very

A Cecil B. De Mille Production. *The Volga Boatman.*
PRINCESS VERA FINDS THAT, DISPERSED, THE PICTURESQUE VOLGA BOATMEN BECOME LITTLE BETTER THAN BEASTS OF BURDEN.

well, then. You don't want to go with the caravan. I'll let them go and I'll stay with you."

And she did. The following morning the rest of her camp left the place. Mariusha came to sit near Ivan in front of Feodor's hut. He had been sleeping in Feodor's hut the last few days, for he had wanted to be with him and talk to him and listen to him all the time. She had a small bundle under her arm which contained all her belongings.

"Where do you sleep?" she asked, "that I may lay my bundle down near your sleeping place."

Feodor stood up and looked at both of them. He was very sad at first, but suddenly he burst out into loud laughter.

"Really," he said to Ivan, "I did not know you had married. But you could not have chosen better. I see no reason for your being so cold. And if you say another word I shall ask her myself to stay here."

His eyes glistened with anticipated pleasure as he spoke.

"That is the kind of a man I like," Mariusha called out, slapping him familiarly on the shoulder. "Tavarish Feodor, you would not have asked me to go away from near you."

And at that moment Ivan knew another thing, that he was jealous. Whether she had done it purposely in order to awaken that feeling in him or it was merely one of her ways it did not matter. He realized he was jealous. He hit her with his fist for the manner in which she had spoken, and cursed her. She laughed, tried to hit Ivan back, and jeered.

"And he is a man of the new order, this moujik."

Mariusha's staying with Ivan at Feodor's camp made an entirely different man of him. The mere sight of two rovers recalled to him all his own roving of the last years. What was there to hold him where he was except the change in his ideas? His gnarled wife scolded and shrieked from early morning till late at night. His grown-up children hardly looked at their father at all, though he was working alongside them and was doing twice the amount of work they were doing in the field. The woman was never satisfied and neither were his sons."

"You owe me years of work," his wife continually shrieked at him. "Years of work. You should work day and night as I have worked to feed your children."

She cursed him. She called him names.

He had borne all her reproaches calmly till then. But Ivan could see immediately that something was changing within him these days.

"Ivan," he told him one day. "Do you think we could get a boat at Nijni Novgorod?"

"I think we could," Ivan answered.

"Ivan," Feodor told him, "if you walk ahead along the shore I shall rejoin you, maybe, in a day or two. We could get to Nijni Novgorod in a week."

Ivan was glad that he had decided to come along. He suspected that Mariusha had something to do with his change of mind, though he was absolutely certain that he was not going to be faithless to him.

He was glad to go because sitting in one place was not in Ivan's blood. Even his great love for Feodor which had held him there for a few weeks could not have lasted much longer in that place.

"Feodor," Ivan told him, "I shall wait for you at Piemitzin, at the inn that is run by the Jew Moishe."

"But that inn isn't going any more," Feodor answered.

"But the house is still there, and it is as good a place to stay as any in the neighborhood. From there we'll only be three days from Nijni."

His eyes lit up.

"We shall pass Kastiri on the way, where the Kniaz Nikita and his family are living now. You know the land has been taken away from them and they are in great fear that something terrible might happen to them. I wonder how it goes with the kniaz's daughter Vera, who used to be such a haughty creature, although she was the kindest of all her brood, running around to the peasants' huts in the winter and helping them with food, always talking to them about the better days to come through education. I had a long talk with her one day. I told her where the source of the festering sore was. She listened very attentively and wanted me to tell her more. But suddenly her father came upon us. He threw himself at me with his whip. She is a very beautiful woman. The kniaz is a crazy, drunken tyrant. I hope to meet her. . . ."

After that Feodor and Ivan kissed longly and renewed their promises of eternal brotherhood. He fought and quarreled with Mariusha when alone. She had kissed Feodor too passionately. She had brought her limbs close against his and the naked calves of her

THE VOLGA BOATMAN 35

legs had twitched as she had kissed him again and again. She laughed at Ivan when he reproached her such behavior. Feodor was a fine fellow. He appreciated her. A woman is to the man who could hold her.

"If you come between us . . ." Ivan threatened her.

She laughed . . .

Ivan's plans of getting rid of Mariusha had vanished as soon as they were again on the road. She had become very much like food that turns a little spicier with time, and though more dangerous to the stomach, more palatable, more tasty. She seemed to pay Ivan less attention than she had paid before, and seemed to care little whether he came along or was left behind. There were moments in which Ivan thought these were merely tactics, womanly wiles to keep him interested. But there were other moments in which he thought that she had really gotten tired of him, that she did not want him any more, and, what was worst of all, that she had had her head turned by Feodor.

The following day they met her people's caravan again. When they camped that night Mariusha sat down near her people, and though Ivan joined them and tried to make himself as useful and important to them as he had been before, it was she who talked to them. And she talked to them in their own language.

A group of roving peasants passed by and made themselves at home near the camp fire of the gypsies. There was a big fellow among them who still wore part of the military uniform, and he was loud-mouthed and foul-mouthed and seemed to be the leader of the band.

"Where are you going, you people?" Ivan asked.

"We are going to look at our Russia," he answered. "It is our Russia now since the Czar has been deposed. We are going to look at it. We haven't seen it. It has been the Czar's Russia till now. From now on it is our Russia."

And setting his eye upon Mariusha, he stared at her, and grinning widely, he said, "And you, you gypsies. You have belonged to the wealthy ones. From now on you are going to belong to us."

Ivan could see that he was getting ready to make himself familiar with her. For the gypsies had gotten thoroughly scared, seeing the number of peasants about them.

THE VOLGA BOATMAN

"We too are Russians," Mariusha's father said.

"You are tzigans. You belong to us," the big brute answered, and the others assented.

And they all came nearer to Mariusha as if she was the one who belonged to them.

"It is my wife," Ivan said to the leader of the band, putting himself in front of Mariusha.

"There does not exist any more such a thing," the brute answered, half drunk with vodka, and drunk with his own sensation of power in words.

But Ivan had grown wild by this time. Putting his hand to the hilt of his knife, he said, "Well, you just try and you'll find out whether it exists or not."

They soon made peace, however, and sat around the fire together. And the peasants were satisfied that the gypsies should sing to them songs, and sing to them the same songs they had sung to kniazes and landlords at the inns and wine houses of the wealthy.

"We are the masters now. We, the moujiks, we are all czars, kniazes. Play, tzigans."

Ivan watched them closely, and watched them even more closely because Mariusha did not seem to be frightened by the prospect of becoming another man's wife if she were to be taken away. When they had gone, early at dawn, he quarreled with Mariusha. And then and there he consecrated her as his wife in the good old Russian fashion by giving her a solid beating. And though she screamed and yelled and cursed, he knew that she was happy. Her tribe merely stood aside, for they too saw in the beating her a sort of consecration, the holy rituals of Russian marriage.

She was a good deal more lovely and subdued after that beating, and they kissed and embraced one another passionately, and Ivan was telling her, "None of these things. You are my wife now, Mariusha. I am the master. Do you hear?"

She pressed herself close to Ivan's bosom as she repeated with her hot breath close to his mouth.

"And I, who thought you no longer loved me. I, who thought that my heart had deceived me. It has deceived me. Ivan, I have only played with you. I only wanted to see whether you loved me, whether I could make you jealous. Ivan, I love you. And if you have never known what the love of a gypsy woman is you shall know from now on. I swear that you shall know, Ivan. But if you ever leave me— If you ever, ever leave me!"

Her words were so warm and sincere that they set his mind at rest. And they made him specially happy because they kept him from suspecting Feodor.

CHAPTER IV

FEODOR joined them sooner than Ivan expected. They had hardly fixed camp the third evening when they heard his call from a distance. He had a little bundle slung over his shoulder, and he was as gay and light-footed as a boy.

"Hurrah," he said. "I am on the road again. And I am happy again."

And he shook hands all around. Ivan called him to sit at the camp fire, and partake of the food the gypsies had unearthed from the bottom of the wagon in which it was hidden. They had hardly finished asking one another about what had happened during the few days of their separation when Mariusha began to tell him how she was beaten by Ivan.

"Ivan," Feodor said, standing up and looking him in the eyes with great anger, "what do you mean by that?"

"She did not behave," he answered.

He looked sternly at Ivan, but immediately broke out in loud laughter.

THE VOLGA BOATMAN

"It is as I thought. You cannot change with laws the nature of things. Didn't you know it was forbidden to beat one's wife now? And that women are equal to men?"

"Ah, what do I care whether it is forbidden or not?" Ivan answered.

Feodor laughed, and slapping Mariusha on the shoulder, he said, "I suppose you now feel yourself more his wife than you ever felt before."

She grinned as she answered, "I do. And God help any one who should try to take him away from now on."

She said this so fiercely that Ivan shuddered. It frightened him to hear her say these words.

Feodor took the reins of the group in his hands. And before the fire had gone down it was he who suggested to the rest of the camp that they go their way and leave Mariusha and Ivan.

"He has married her only," he said, "and not the whole tribe. No good will come of sticking all together. It will make traveling so much more difficult. And besides, as soon as we reach Nijni we intend to go back to our old occupation of boat pulling. The Volga is calling us. What can we do with you? Her we can keep in the boat on the way while we are pulling it along the shore. We cannot drag you with us."

"And then," he said to them, "you will have to look for something else to make your living by. There will be no more gold thrown into your fiddles by kniazes and boyars. Those days are gone. You'll have to work at other things from now on than the things at which you have worked. And the sooner you learn that the better. You shall shoe horses for a living and play only when the spirit moves you; play for yourself and friends."

There was loud crying and wailing that night. They quarreled amongst themselves, the gypsies, instead of sitting down to decide calmly what to do. And whenever they came over to talk to Mariusha in "calo" she shrugged her shoulders as if it did not concern her what happened to them. She had at one stroke separated herself from them and did not seem to care what they were doing. It is so with all women. Man never separates himself completely from the nest in which he was born. When a woman only thinks of making her own nest she has already abandoned that of her brood. And it is that for which a woman never forgives a man, that he still clings to the old nest.

THE VOLGA BOATMAN 43

In the morning Mariusha's father begged that they should still remain together until Nijni Novgorod. There he had many friends. He feared to travel alone before then. Every one questioned them on the road.

"From where? When? How?"

Feodor agreed rather reluctantly to let them come part of the way, and accepted the bargain only after a big bottle of vodka had emerged from the recesses of one of the wagons. He had not had any drink for a long time, and a big gulp down the gullet shook him up considerably and made him act in a strange way. It made him want to preach again as he had preached before. He jumped up on the end of the wagon and began to talk to the gypsies of the great days ahead, of the morrow, forgetting completely that these great days had already arrived and that he had already realized himself that they were not as great as he had thought them to be.

The gypsies listened open-mouthed. Mariusha seemed to take it all in. And the more Feodor drank the more he preached. They had to stop several times on the way, for he insisted on speaking at the crossroads where the peasants from the neighborhood assembled. Open-mouthed, awe-struck, the peasants listened to him. Never before had they heard such fiery speech. Never before had they heard such a clear-cut exposition of the happiness in store for them. That was it. That man knew. He told them. Yes. Yes. Do you hear what he says?

When he was through with one speech, and after Ivan had almost forced him to get into the carriage to drive on ahead, the people surrounded them to ask questions. They wanted to know, and he seemed to be the only man who could tell them all about it.

"Feodor," Ivan begged him, "won't you leave the bottle with me?"

But he had the bottle in one of the pockets of his fur coat, and would not separate himself from it. He drank sparingly after the first few gulps, in fear that it might come to an end, as if it was the last bottle of vodka on earth, of which he was the sole possessor. But he drank so slowly and tasted every drop so thoroughly that the little he drank had the same effect on him as if he had drunk great quantities.

There was a lot of truth in what he said when he spoke to the peasants, and there was a lot of it which Ivan believed much more than Feodor did, although Feodor was the speaker. For Ivan knew all the things he had told him, all his disappointments and disillusionments which he seemed to forget as he was carried along by the sound of his own voice and by the heat of his own arguments. Ivan was already thinking of the reaction in him when he should sober up. Ivan was also thinking that while these men listened to talk of better days they were doing nothing to bring them about. The country lacked food. They grew nothing. They were half naked. The women talked. The looms were idle. The peasants butchered their oxen instead of working in the fields with them and then listened to talk and more talk.

That evening before the stars were out they arrived in front of Kniaz Nikita's castle. Either because the peasants still feared the kniaz or because the kniaz had shrewdly accepted part of the theories that floated abroad, the village of people around the kniaz's castle seemed not to have been disturbed by all that had happened in Russia. Theoretically the land belonged to the peasants. Feodor, still drunk with his own speeches and with the vodka that he had swallowed, tried to gather people around him on the crossroads to speak to them. But they turned cold shoulders. They were uninterested in what he had to say.

It angered Feodor. Instead of trying to convince people he pinned them against walls and fences as he approached them, and compelled them to listen to him. The peasants now feared to oppose him openly because he spoke what the new government seemed to want everybody to say. They had been told that the Jews had gotten hold of Russia and sold it to the Niemtzias. They listened peaceably and nodded their heads. Some of them even took their fur caps off their heads as they did to kniazes and government officers. But they would not say a word and kept their own minds.

It enraged Feodor more and more as the thing went on.

"Drive on to the castle," he told the gypsies.

"Why? What for?" Ivan interfered, trying to stop the procession. "Feodor, what has possessed you? Now, let us talk the matter over. Just for a while."

But Feodor would not listen to his friend.

"Drive on to the castle. I want to see what is happening there. I want to see how the kniaz's daughter Vera is behaving now, that haughty dame. How the Czar's own little cousin is behaving now. Do they know there has been a revolution? He has come upon me with his whip when I talked to his daughter."

"It must be a nest of reaction, the kniaz's castle," Feodor went on. "It must be a nest of hundreds of people who have fled from all parts of Russia to await there their opportunity to overthrow the present government and bring back the old. He has struck me with his whip. Now we are the masters. I shall make him tremble before me."

All Feodor's old fire seemed to return. He was beyond himself with rage as he spoke.

Ivan took a drink himself from the bottle after that, and he took another drink after the first. It was good vodka, strong vodka, and he had not had any in his mouth for a long time.

"Yea, to the kniaz's castle," he joined Feodor's cry. "Drive on to the kniaz's castle. There must be some very pretty daughters of kniazes there. We shall make them dance. We shall make them sing."

And the gypsies were willing to go where they were asked. Mariusha watched the two men quietly, but with great interest, and her people watched her for a decision.

And as they jogged along, sitting on the rear end of one of the cars, Feodor said to Ivan, "But the kniaz's house you must leave to me. I have a good mind to marry his daughter and carry her along on top of the barges as I shall pull them along. That will be a great thing. I do not want my other wife any more. Ha! Ha! I am a revolutionist. This is the new order of things."

They laughed and joked about that, and pretty soon they were at the outside fences of the kniaz's palace. But the fences were still intact. Elsewhere where they had passed by houses of landlords the fences had been torn down. There had been windows that had been smashed and torn from their hinges, and doors that had been broken in. But Kniaz Nikita's house was intact, the fences still standing up, the windows in their places, and there was light everywhere. There seemed to be some sort of feast going on within.

CHAPTER V

Feodor and Ivan knocked at the gate, which was immediately opened, and they were allowed inside. Instinctively Ivan took his cap off, but Feodor would not have it so. He insisted that Ivan put his cap back.

"Let them uncover themselves before us," he said as he pushed Ivan's cap back on his head.

There were more reasons than one why Ivan should fear to be in the presence of Kniaz Nikita. There were things he remembered about him. There were things he had heard people tell about him and his father and his grandfather.

Feodor was the first one to break through the peasant servants in the halls. Soon they were in a large room where there were about twenty people about the table, all in great earnestness. They were all dressed in Russian peasant costumes, and it was only with great difficulty that Ivan distinguished the kniaz and the people of his own kind from the peasants that were there.

"Good evening, tavarishe," Feodor called out to them.

"Good evening, tavarish," Kniaz Nikita answered after a few seconds, during which the other people looked at one another, not knowing how to answer to the greeting or how to receive the intruders.

"I do not know whether you have mesmerized the people here or whether the people here are all traitors to our present government," Feodor addressed the kniaz, who had risen to his feet.

The peasants bowed their heads. They felt like traitors, and they had heard of the terrible things that the present government did to those who were not faithful to it. They turned around and looked at the two men with frightened eyes.

"We are neither traitors nor fools," Kniaz Nikita answered as his face grew red. "We are good Russians, and we are doing as we see fit."

"Russians? You Russians!" Feodor repeated, and began to laugh. "There is not enough Russian blood in you to fill a spider's stomach. The only Russian blood in you is what you have sucked from the people."

A few youngsters with refined faces detached themselves from the group of peasants and stood aside. And Ivan could see from the manner in which they wore the Russian costume that it was a long time indeed since they had worn it, if they had ever worn it at all. The kniaz's daughter came up and looked Feodor up and down. And suddenly she burst out in loud laughter.

"As I live, it is the boatman Feodor, the one who used to sing so well. And look at him now, the way he speaks and talks."

She was beautiful indeed. A different kind of beauty from Mariusha's. She turned around and winked at one of the men. And instantly several bottles of vodka appeared on the table. She had scented Feodor's weakness.

Yet before the bottles had been brought up Feodor, for whom her presence seemed to be an even greater incitement to talk, jumped up on the table and began to address the peasants about him. He had never spoken before with such enthusiasm, with such warmth, such conviction.

At first the peasants listened to him in a more or less perfunctory way, as if they had been compelled to listen to the voice of some popa. But his words and his voice intoxicated them. His arguments swayed them. They began to look at one another questioningly, and looked at the kniaz and his group of people as if to ask them, "Well, what have you to say to that?"

Then they began to murmur and assent, as if what Feodor was telling them was just expressing the very depths of their own souls. And Feodor was talking on and on, refusing several times the glass that Vera brought to him as he was standing on the table in seeming derision of all he said.

"Wet your lips, brother," she said, "that they may not dry uttering such wisdom. Come, wet your lips that you may have an excuse for such drunken talk."

He pushed the glass gently away from him and went on talking. She offered it to him again a little later on.

"Drink another glass. It is of the same kind in which you have found your wisdom."

He refused it again, gently pushing it from him.

Then one of the peasants said to her, "Tavarisha Vera Ivanovna, leave the man alone. Do not disturb him. What he says may or may not be to your liking. Yet it is true."

The kniaz and the few young men shivered

THE VOLGA BOATMAN 53

from head to foot that one of their own men should address the kniaz's daughter as "tavarisha." It meant the beginning of the conversion of their people to something they hated and detested.

And after Feodor had spoken a little longer the peasants began to look at the other group which had separated itself from them. The two groups edged away from one another slowly, forming two distinct camps, like water separating itself from oil. The peasants now began to be won over to Feodor's side. One could see in what passed through their eyes and in their gestures that they were ready to turn on their erstwhile protectors, that their eyes had been opened by Feodor. And knowing his Russians, Ivan dreaded the violence that was to follow. For he hated violence. He always hated violence. He could imagine them going out and breaking down fences and doors and windows, as if in breaking down they were saving themselves and saving Russia from destruction.

Ivan went out, called to Mariusha, and asked her to call in her people, and that they bring their fiddles with them. Ivan put his arms about Feodor, who was still talking.

"Tavarish," he said to him, "Feodor, you

are getting tired. The people here are not going to run away. We are all of the same mind. Why can't we sit down here in the kniaz's own house and have our meal, and have some music and some songs? There is Mariusha here, and she is willing to sing."

Well, it is the way of the Russians. You can easily sway them from one thing to another if you but say the right word at the right time. We are a people of words. We are a people of moods. We are a people that will slave for the man or the woman that utters the right word at the right time. And we are always eager for drink and song. And Ivan had said the right word at the right time. Feodor clambered down from the table.

"Yea, let's hear some song," the peasants said.

And one of the peasants, who had been the first to be convinced, called out, "Let the same gypsies who used to play for the kniaz and his people only, play for us now."

"Tune your fiddles, tzigans," they called out.

"Wait," Ivan interfered. "They are tavarishes just as you are. And this is my wife."

Ivan could see by looking at Feodor, that having sobered up through his long winded

THE VOLGA BOATMAN

speeches, he was beginning to fear the consequences of what his own words might stir up. Now that the peasants grew a little louder and wilder Feodor began to counsel them.

"Now, brothers, I want no violence. I want no destruction. Let's understand one another. But you mustn't break up things. We mustn't destroy things. If all this belongs to us we don't want to destroy it. It is ours. If you destroy it you acknowledge that it does not belong to you."

But even as he spoke things from about the room disappeared under the fur coats of the peasants. Silver candelabras, samovars, pieces of glassware, little mirrors that hung about the rooms. And Vera's own sable coat, which had hung over a chair, had suddenly disappeared from where it was, while the kniaz and his people were looking at one another alarmed and frightened at what might happen next.

"No, no, there will be no destruction," the long-bearded peasants said to one another. "No. No. But this is ours. It belongs to us, does it not?"

There were several women among the peasants, and they began to finger pieces of silk that hung about the furniture in the house, and the velvet hangings on the windows. Bottles of vodka that had been on the table were opened, and they were now looking around for food and addressing the woman of the house.

"Tavarisha Vera," they asked her. "Tavarisha, isn't there any zakuska about the house? We are hungry. There must be some zakuska right near the place from where you have taken the vodka. Tell us, tavarisha, where have you taken the vodka from?"

A few of them pressed closer as they asked, "Tell us, tavarisha, where you have taken the vodka from. Now, Tavarish Kniaz Nikita, tell your daughter to tell us where the vodka has been taken from."

And when one or two of the young men edged closer to disengage the kniaz and his daughter from the surrounding mob, which had grown larger, for people were coming in continually, another mob surrounded them, and leeringly and grinningly asked:

"Tell the kniaz, tavarish, to tell his daughter to tell us where the vodka has been taken from, that we may find some zakuska near by. They don't have to disturb themselves to go get it. We shall do that ourselves. We want some zakuska."

"Feodor," Ivan said, walking up to him.

"You have swayed them this way. Sway them now the other way, or there'll be murder within a few moments. You have lit the match, now put out the fire. For God's sake put out the fire before it's too late."

He had grown pale and he was trembling. He was bewildered by what was happening about him, seeing the insistence with which the people pressed upon the kniaz and his daughter to be told where the vodka was.

"Quiet now," Ivan called, "that my friends may play."

The kniaz winked at his daughter. Laughingly she turned around and taunted the people.

"Why, you give me no chance to answer you. You keep on asking me a question without giving me a chance to say where the vodka is. Of course you can have whatever vodka is left in the house. It is all yours. Here is the key to the cellar, and you will find some zakuska there. But bring it all up here that we may all eat and drink together in peace. If it is yours it is also ours. Aren't we Russians all alike? And if there are things here in the house that you like, why steal them and carry them under your shubas like thieves instead of asking for them, or merely taking them openly; since we are tavarishe and everything belongs to all of us there may be such things I also like. Come, be brothers. This is the great revolution. Everything belongs to everybody, not only to those to whom it has not belonged before."

She spoke sarcastically as she looked at both Ivan and Feodor.

"Feodor," Ivan said, "can't you stop them?"

Feodor got up and tried to interfere, but it had evidently gone beyond him and he was powerless to do so.

"Play," Ivan turned around to his gypsy friends. "Play. Play on."

They struck up a lively tune, and Ivan made them play it even in a livelier way than it was usually played. Then he urged Mariusha on to sing. She looked at him. She was reluctant. But when he repeated the order, she sang. It was the kamarashka, a tune every Russian from one end of the country to the other knows and responds to. Within a few minutes all the peasants had joined in the song. And when the others had returned from the cellar with several loaves of bread, and hams, and chunks of dried meat and fish, as well as armfuls of bottles which they brought from the cellar and piled upon the

THE VOLGA BOATMAN 59

table, every soul joined in the song and dance. Kniaz Nikita himself seemed to be as gay as the rest, and his daughter, now acting good-naturedly as the hostess, cut the chunks of meat for the peasants and filled the glasses.

"Drink, brothers. Eat, brothers."

It was wonderful how she took her rôle, and Ivan admired her for that. She helped avoid bloodshed. It was good breeding that did it all, good Russian breeding.

But the refined youngsters of the nobility who were in the room did not take the play so readily. They remained outside the circle, gritting their teeth, glaring savagely, and were not to be dragged into the dance, even when the kniaz himself danced as abandonedly as any of the peasants, pounding his heavy boots on the floor as he danced to the kamarashka, calling the others about him.

"Tavarish, tavarish. Come, sing, drink, dance."

Feodor took one glass after another. Vera was serving him. And every time she served him he looked deep into her eyes, again trying to find courage and his old faith in vodka.

"You are beautiful," he told her.

And she laughed and turned away with dancing eyes.

"Feodor," Ivan begged, putting his hand on the man's glass, "haven't you had enough?"

But he shook Ivan off and insisted that he, too, should have a drink with him.

"She is so beautiful, so beautiful," he repeated.

One drink after another, one drink after another, and Ivan was soon as drunk as any of them.

The gypsies played, but they also were drinking heavily, and their dances and their songs were jogging along. Peasants fell down dancing, and stumbled over one another, leaning against one another, leaning against the wall, and sagging against it, grumbling, cursing, uttering snatches of song and muttering bits of the speech that they had heard a while ago from Feodor's lips. It was with great effort that Ivan kept his eyes open.

"Feodor," he muttered, half conscious, "can't you stop them?"

But Feodor himself was beyond control. His eyes were riveted on Vera, who attracted him and fascinated him. And through the mist that clouded Ivan's mind he heard him say to her:

"There are no more kniazes. I am as good

THE VOLGA BOATMAN 61

as you are. There are no more kniazes, no more nobility."

And he put his arms about her, pulling her towards him to kiss her. She cried out.

And then a shot rang out. The noise sobered Ivan up instantly. It had done the same thing to a number of the peasants, who suddenly jumped up from the floor. The lights had gone out almost at the same moment.

"Let everybody stand where he is," Ivan yelled out in the darkness, fully master of himself.

Some one struck a match. Ivan rolled part of a hanging in his hand, which he lit, and then looked around. Feodor was lying in the middle of the room. His eyes rolled once or twice and remained fixed like two pieces of glass. A thin stream of blood was running behind them.

"Make light," Ivan ordered Vera.

She pressed a button somewhere, for the kniaz's house was lit by electricity. Feodor was dead. Ivan looked around, ready to spring like a tiger on the man who had killed him, and tear him to pieces. But the young people he had watched from the very beginning of the performance had disappeared.

The peasants uncovered their heads.

And then one of them called out: "So they have killed him! So they have killed him! He who had spoken to us about life. He who had been one of ours has been killed! They have killed him. Death to the murderers!"

A Cecil B. De Mille Production. *The Volga Boatman.*
LEADING THE BAND OF REVOLUTIONISTS, FEODOR INVADES THE CASTLE OF PRINCE NIKITA AND HIS DAUGHTER.

CHAPTER VI

An implacable hatred towards the kniaz and the youngsters who had run away and the kniaz's daughter seized Ivan's heart. So that was why they had brought drink here! That was why they had urged the people on to drink and to dance? That they should be able to kill his Feodor at will. His Feodor. His Feodor. And he, who had not trusted all Feodor had said while he was alive, suddenly began to believe everything that he had said, now that he was dead, and believe it even more firmly than he could ever have believed it himself.

Ivan looked at the peasants, and it seemed to him that they too felt likewise, that they too felt that one of theirs had been killed by one of the others, and that he who killed one of theirs was their implacable enemy. All his doubts as to the ability of peasants governing themselves vanished, and he understood even more than Feodor that they had a right to govern themselves if such people had been their masters. His dead body spoke a stronger language than his living body had ever been able to speak. It was not as much a government by the people that the people needed, but revenge for all the things that had been done to them. And it was what Ivan also wanted, revenge.

"Close the doors," he called, not knowing why.

He wanted these two people there, the kniaz and his daughter, the only ones of the others that had remained in the room, that they should answer with their lives for the life of Feodor.

"Two men after the murderers," Ivan ordered, never looking whether his order was executed or not.

And then he looked at them. The old kniaz was bewildered. It was pitiful to see him. He looked like an animal that had been caught in a trap. His furtive eyes ran about the house like the eyes of a mouse. He wanted to talk to the peasants, but they had bowed and bared their heads in awe before the dead one, and they looked at him like terrible avengers. Their good-natured faces suddenly changed into faces of intense hatred. They had so suddenly awakened from the stupor of their drunkenness that they were like bears that had suddenly been shaken into life before the hibernation was over.

The kniaz began to speak to them. "A fool, the one who has killed your tavarish. Let's go after him. Let's all go after them. Come."

But Ivan knew that it was only a pretext to get out of the room, to gain time during which to appease the angry peasants, or to run away. The one who had killed Feodor was by this time probably far away on horseback, and there was no earthly use running after him. The peasants were drunk. They were horseless.

"It is not only one man who has killed our tavarish," Ivan cried, stopping the kniaz from talking further. "It is one of yours. And one of yours will soon lie near my dear dead friend," he said, pointing at Feodor. "And I am going to avenge him."

And the peasants, now shaking themselves together, grouping themselves in a circle around the kniaz and his daughter, said, "Yea, one of yours, one of you two is going to lie down there beside him."

Their hands stretched out ready to tear the two limb from limb.

And one peasant cried out: "For hundreds of years you have killed us thus. For hundreds of years you have persecuted us and driven us and destroyed us. The kniaz, your father, killed my oldest brother because he hunted in your forest and killed a deer, out of which he fed his wife and children."

And another peasant cried out, "And the kniaz, your father, has whipped one of mine almost to death because he had taken a sheep from your fold. And you, Nikita, who have killed our tavarish, what haven't you done to our maidens? And now, when one of ours has but wanted to steal a kiss you have killed him."

The kniaz's daughter then began to talk. "Aren't you ashamed, Russians, to talk that way to your kniaz? Aren't you ashamed to talk that way to my father after all the things I have done for you?"

But Ivan did not let her speak.

"You have talked enough," he said. He was in a terrible drunken mood. "One of you two will have to lie down beside him. And I am going to do it. A life for a life. And Feodor's life is going to be avenged by me. By me. By me. I loved him. He was more than a brother to me. He belonged to all of us. He was a Russian."

It was a sight to see Mariusha breaking

through and throwing herself at the body of Feodor. She cried and wept and carried on. And when she jumped to her feet again it was with both hands at the throat of Vera; as if Vera had killed the one she liked.

"You have murdered him," she cried.

Ivan threw her aside. "I give you five minutes to decide which one of you will die," he said to the kniaz and his daughter. "You can talk it over between yourselves while we are standing in the other corner."

The peasants agreed. "Yes, let them decide which of the two shall die."

The two were left in one corner of the room. Ivan imposed silence while he cleaned out the revolver that Mariusha had handed him from one of the innumerable folds of her dress.

He took out the watch which had fallen out from one of Feodor's pockets. It ticked away, living while Feodor was dead. It made Ivan cry. At first Vera and her father fell into one another's arms weeping loudly. But Ivan's heart did not soften. When he thought the hearts of the peasants were softening he cried out:

"Let them weep. Our people have wept long enough. For centuries we have wept. And has anybody paid any attention to our weeping? Has anybody paid any attention to our tears?"

"He is right. What he says is true," the peasants said.

And then he heard the kniaz's voice breaking into sobs after they had whispered to one another, and his own heart began to soften. Then he recalled a tale of the neighborhood, how the father of the kniaz, because a widow's child had kicked one of his dogs, had ordered the widow and her child and the whole of his village to come to the castle, and there in the presence of all he ordered the mother that she strip the little boy naked. Then he ordered the widow to take the white little body, which had been flesh of her flesh, to a little distance and he called to the child to run. And as the child ran, while the mother was away from it, the fierce dogs the kniaz always kept in his kennels were let loose upon it. At the sight of what happened the peasants fled in all directions. Years later the mother of that child, with a bundle of rags in her arms, wandered through the villages, insane, telling the story and how she had rescued the child; and she showed the bundle of rags.

Two minutes were up. Ivan grew impatient. The gun in his hand trembled. His whole body shook together with it. He groped for one of the bottles and poured a long drink to steady himself. He wanted to be over with it. He was afraid of weakening.

"Have you decided which one is going to lie down near Feodor?" Ivan called out.

Vera came forward. "I will lie down beside him if that is your will," she said fiercely. "If that is your Christian desire."

"You have talked enough, woman," he answered.

"It is better that I die than be left a prey to beasts like you," she answered, "after my father is dead."

"You have talked enough, woman," Ivan answered again.

"You can do no worse than kill me," she said fiercely, "and I shall talk to the last moment if it pleases me to talk, moujik."

"Let her talk now," some of the peasants called out, softened by her impertinence and by her courage.

"Why shouldn't he kill the kniaz?" another one said. "Why should it be said that we have killed a woman? Kill the kniaz."

"I have given them the choice," Ivan answered. "And it is up to them to decide which one is to die."

And as he said that he saw in the eyes of the younger peasants that it would have been no good for Vera to remain alive if her father was to pay for the life of Feodor. They all lusted for her, with a strange lust, as if possessing her body would have avenged them for the many maidens the kniazes had possessed against their wills.

"Kill her, the viper," Mariusha now said, "for she was the one who fired the shot at Feodor. I swear she was the one."

Again Mariusha made an attempt to jump at Vera's throat and again Ivan pulled her aside.

"Stay where you are," he ordered her, "or you will soon know who is master."

The kniaz came forward and pleaded with Vera that she allow him to die. His voice faltered, his knees were sagging. He was trembling all over while Vera was unafraid and erect. Though he begged her to let him die in her place, he was not as willing as his words were. He had trained himself for so long to have his lips say what his heart never intended that even now he did the same.

Vera pacified him. "It is better that I should die than be their prey after you are dead," she said.

"So that is decided," Ivan told Vera. "That is decided. You will die."

"I will," she answered.

"All out," he ordered. "And when you are out close the doors and the shutters of the windows and stay outside."

They all filed out. Some gayly, others like after a sermon in the church.

Ivan found a candle in one of the heavy brass candlesticks over the mantelpiece. He lit it and stuck it in one of the empty bottles on the table. They were alone, Vera and Ivan. There was a flickering, unsteady light. Only the pale hands and the white face of the young woman were visible in the flickering light. Her eyes gleamed in the semi-darkness. The rest of her merged and melted into the shadows of the dark room.

"I give you five minutes now to make your prayers," Ivan said to her, "and get yourself ready."

"And is that what you call government by the people?" she asked, coming nearer. Ivan could feel her breath in his face. It was steady, warm and deep. There was no tremor in her voice. It was full of anger and sarcasm.

"Woman, stay away. A half minute is gone. You are having another four and a half minutes to live."

"And just because a fool has killed your friend you want to take another life! Just because a fool in a moment of insanity has pulled a trigger against your friend you want in cold blood to do the same against me," she said. "Do you think he would have wanted you to do that? Ask him."

She leaned over the dead body.

"If you say another word—" Ivan said, pointing the gun at her, for he was getting nervous and unsettled, "I shall end it all now."

She withdrew to the other end of the room and Ivan took drink after drink to steady himself. The first minute of the five was over. It was both too slow and too fast. And at that moment it seemed to Ivan that he was about to die in another few minutes; that the term he had set for Vera was also the term he had set for himself. He looked at the watch. The seconds were loud, as if they shrieked, "Another second has gone away from your life. Another one. Another one. Say your prayers. You are going to die."

THE VOLGA BOATMAN

Ivan could hardly look again at the watch. He took another drink. She came nearer to him.

"Here is a drink for you. Drink one. Steady yourself."

Vera pushed the drink away.

"I do not need it. I can die. I am not afraid. But you, you—"

"Take it just the same," Ivan told her.

She took a sip.

"You have trapped yourself," she told Ivan. "You have trapped yourself. And now you have to kill me whether you want to kill me or not; just because you have said to these stupid peasants that you are going to kill me. See how you tremble. See how you shake. Which of us two is more afraid? Ha! Ha!"

At that moment Mariusha began to sing outside. The gypsies began to play. And they played the kamarashka again. It sounded not as if four were playing, but as if five hundred had suddenly began to play. They had lost patience, the peasants outside, and they could wait no longer. And it was Mariusha who had started to sing and to play, to make them forget what was going on inside. Probably some one was beginning to talk and to soften them, showing them that they would all commit murder, that it was murder to kill an innocent woman to avenge a murder done by a fool. Perhaps the kniaz had been talking to them.

But Mariusha, cruel Mariusha, she would not let such an occasion pass by. She hated Vera. She hated Vera. She hated her with a hatred woman seems incapable of.

And the dance was getting gayer and gayer outside. And the song was louder. Suddenly Vera stood up, and raising one of her shoulders higher than the other, she began to glide in the room to the rhythm of the music played outside. Her feet raised from the ground, at first a little heavily, but then they gained swing, and she began to turn rapidly around the table at which he sat.

What a marvelous creature! And she was going to die in another two minutes. In another two minutes this being, so courageous, was going to lie still even as Feodor was lying still on the floor.

"Stop," Ivan called to her. "Stop your dancing."

But she only laughed at him, grinned, and began to dance with even greater abandon to the increased rhythm outside. For the peas-

THE VOLGA BOATMAN 75

ants, too, were dancing furiously. The kniaz was in their midst and they were dancing around him, forcing him to dance.

"Stop," Ivan called again to Vera, pointing the gun at her.

"What Russian can stop dancing to the kamarashka? What Russian can keep her feet still when the kamarashka is being played? Why don't you dance?" she called, leering. "I have two more minutes, you say. I want to dance them away."

And even while she talked she never stopped dancing. She danced, and the words she said just burned themselves into Ivan.

"What Russian could stop dancing when the kamarashka was played?" she had said.

And there was her executioner, with a revolver ready in his hand to kill the fellow Russian who could not resist dancing the kamarashka. Two minutes before dying!

He poured himself another drink, and another drink. That watch was ticking too rapidly. And he looked at her again. She was beautiful. She danced so marvelously. She had thrown one hand behind her neck and was dancing with the greatest abandon. Ivan's hand trembled on the gun.

"Kneel down and pray," he told her. "You have one more minute."

"One more minute," she repeated. "I hope they don't stop playing."

And then a thousand thoughts flitted through Ivan's mind. So this was it! This new life of which he had heard so much. This new order of things of which other people had spoken and which Ivan had only half believed till then, and in which Feodor's body had inspired him to believe more than he wanted. It was Russian killing Russian. What mattered it whether it was kniaz killing peasant or peasant killing kniaz? One was as cruel as the other, one as vengeful as the other, kniaz or peasant. Vera was not only the kniaz's daughter. She was a Russian. She was not able to keep her feet still at a Russian dance, even a few minutes before she was to die. Her heart and soul had answered to the same tune as his had answered to many a time. As the souls and hearts of the people outside had answered to the tune Mariusha was playing. As millions of other hearts would answer, as millions of other feet would rise and dance. They were of the same blood, and just because a fool had killed Feodor—just because a fool had killed Feodor— Another half minute.

THE VOLGA BOATMAN

"Is my time up?" she asked. "I am getting tired," she said, dancing and coming nearer to Ivan.

He poured a drink for her. "Have a drink," he asked.

But she pushed the glass away from her. "I don't need one. You need it. Take it yourself," she said, holding the glass to his mouth.

There were just a few seconds before the five minutes were up, and the music outside stopped suddenly, the deep silence was broken only by the sobs of an old man. And suddenly Ivan heard Mariusha's voice.

"Hey, the time is up. The time is up. Pull your trigger."

But at that moment Ivan would sooner have shot the bullet through Mariusha's heart than through the heart of the Russian woman near him. There was another silence after that, and then Mariusha's call, accompanied by the feeble voice of a few men outside, came again.

"The time is up. Pull the trigger, tavarish."

Ivan raised the gun and Vera stood up facing him, looking him in the eyes. He put it to her heart and closed his eyes. He could not pull the trigger. He opened his eyes again. He half expected to see her leer provokingly. It would have given him an excuse to pull the trigger in anger. But she looked calmly, pityingly, as if it were Ivan who was to die and not her. And then again it came to Ivan, she had danced to the kamarashka. She had responded to the same tune as he responded, as the whole Russian people responded.

Mariusha's call came for the third time that the time was up. Several fists were beating against the door. And a sudden decision came to Ivan. Only half knowing what he was doing, he pulled the trigger, but with the gun pointing to the ceiling. The door was burst open. Pell-mell the crowd rushed in. He carried Vera, who was half fainting in his arms, beating his way through with the hand holding the gun and kicking with his feet.

She was lying still in his arms and he could hear the peasants yell, "He is going to throw her in the river."

But Mariusha's voice rose above that of the peasants, and she yelled, "The traitor. He has not killed her. The traitor! After him. Let's kill the two of them. After them, tavarishes."

And she ran after Ivan as he was running

as fast as his feet could move toward the gypsy wagon to which the horses were still harnessed. He got to the wagon first. He whipped the horses. The peasants ran after them, waving their arms in the air. Mariusha and her people followed at top speed, crying, cursing.

CHAPTER VII

NEITHER of them said a word for a long time. All Ivan wanted was to put distance between them and the castle. He knew that the gypsies would lead the band, that there would be a double purpose in their chase, Mariusha's revengeful heart, and the fact that they had stolen the gypsy horses, which they would want to recover at any price. It was indeed lucky that Ivan had gone through the same region so many times, and knew every path, every road, every lane. It was lucky indeed that the horses were as fast as they were. And Ivan knew that the peasants would not allow the gypsies to take any of their horses in fear that they might lose their horses once the gypsies were upon them. He knew that they would be too busy looting the kniaz's palace now that their spirit of revenge had been aroused, that the spirit of loot had been stirred. Now Ivan was a traitor, an even greater criminal than the man who had killed Feodor. For he had betrayed them, and betrayed the dead one, and betrayed the whole class to which they imagined they belonged. When he stopped the horses an hour later he saw clouds of smoke and tongues of fire in the distance. And he knew.

Yet even as he sat beside Vera and felt the warmth of her body Ivan knew that they belonged to two different classes. That they were still enemies though he had saved her life. That the others who were pursuing and were ready to kill him were much nearer to Ivan than she was. In a general way they were all Russians, all people of the same blood, all people of the same ancestry.

At a little village he stopped the horses again, for they were exhausted. And several peasants approached. When they questioned a little too closely Ivan's origin he bared his chest and showed them the sign where the rope had bitten into the flesh across it. It satisfied them.

"And who is she?" they asked.

"My wife," Ivan answered.

They must have wondered about that, for they shook their heads in an incredulous way. Vera was too well dressed to be the wife of a man such as Ivan was. Yet they did not bother. They shook their heads but did not interfere more.

They traveled on again. Before nightfall they came to another little village. And again peasants stopped them, asking the point of destination. Where were they driving so hurriedly?

"My wife's mother lives at Jaroslav and she is very ill. And so she is going to see her before she dies."

"But Jaroslav is in the hands of the anti-revolutionists now," some one said.

"And whence do you come?" they asked.

Ivan told them his place of origin.

"And how is it in your village?" they again inquired.

In a few minutes all his old spirit was aroused. He was in the midst of a circle, and he outspoke them all. And what he said he believed more than ever before. And what he said about the landlords and the exploitation by the kniazes and the government and the boyars bit deeper than anything he had ever said before. He was speaking even as Feodor would have spoken, even as Feodor would have liked him to speak. And a hundred times during his speech he felt like crying out:

"This woman is not my wife. This woman is the daughter of one who has made you suffer for so many ages hunger and cold, who has persecuted you and beaten you and killed you."

But she had danced the kamarashka. Her soul had answered to the same tune his had answered to. To kill her would be to kill a part of himself. And there she was, part of Ivan that he hated and could not destroy, for in destroying it he would have destroyed himself.

"And where are you going?" the peasants asked again.

And when he told them they answered, "But that part is in the hands of the Whites. Who knows but even at this moment there is a traitor in our midst who is going to tell them all you have said? They will back you up against a wall and shoot you the minute you fall into their hands. Russia is full of traitors."

And then they looked at one another searchingly, each one suspecting the other of being a traitor to his own cause.

"There are traitors everywhere amongst us," another peasant said. "It is a land full of traitors."

But Ivan maintained that he could find his way. It was absolutely necessary that his wife should be at her mother's side as soon as possible.

"Let God be with you," one of the peasants answered.

"But why a man should endanger his life for a woman is more than I know. Have you not heard in your village that women are now no longer the subjects of man, that they are even as we are? If she wants to go to see her mother why don't you let her go and see her alone? Why should you endanger your life for her, Tavarish?"

"It is what I have begged him," Vera now interfered. "It is what I have asked him to do. Why should he? Perhaps it is as you say. And the Whites would seize him and kill him, while they would let me pass, for I could tell them and prove to them that I was going to see my mother, my own people. You are right. It is not his mother, but mine. Not his people but mine."

And she took advantage of the opinion of the peasants and pressed further the argument, until for Ivan to maintain his original attitude and insist that he must accompany her to the other side would have betrayed them to the peasants. They all took her part now.

THE VOLGA BOATMAN

"See, women have become independent. It was good of you to bring her so far, but from now on let her take her own way. What are you afraid of?" the peasants said. "If she should not come back in time you will take another wife."

"Give her time to return, and if she does not return in that time, you will take another wife," another man answered. "Let the woman go where she wants. Why should you put your neck in a noose?"

Vera spoke even more eloquently. "He has been so good to me. You don't know how good he has been to me. And I should hate to see him endanger his life just because of a caprice of mine. You do not know how good he has been to me. It is I who tremble for his life, now that you explain the dangers he might encounter. You are right, men. All I want of him is that he let me have the wagon and the horses. He may stay here if he cares, or wait for me wherever he wants. And after I have seen my mother and all is well I will return again, or he may return home."

"Let her go, let her go," the peasants said. "You stay here with us. We need men like you in our midst. We need men like you to deal with traitors when traitors appear."

Ivan thought rapidly. It was perhaps the best way out. On the other side where the Whites were, where the people of her own kind were still trying to get hold of the land and the government, she would be in peace. She would be sheltered by them and no longer in danger of being caught and destroyed by the people we had fled from. And it would also be much easier for him to disappear in the multitude alone than with her. He had encumbered himself. As long as he was with her he felt a traitor to his own people and felt that he should be judged by them as such. He did not know in what manner he could explain, should an explanation be necessary, his saving her life instead of shooting her to avenge Feodor. It would be much easier to be alone.

"So be it," Ivan said. "Let her go."

He went outside to talk to her. But there was not a word he could say.

"I have heard them call you Ivan," she told him. "Ivan, it is better that we go each our own way. Your action has proven to me that you are a Russian. I do not ask you to join me and go over to the other side. You believe that your side may be able to make the Russians happier than they are. I believe that you are wrong, just as you possibly believe that I am wrong. But we are brothers. We shall kill one another trying to make one another happy. I can see that you will be fighting on one side, while I shall fight on the other side; not for a Russia that has been, and not for a Russia as you want it to be, but for a Russia between the two. And what you have done for me I shall never forget. For I shall always feel that what you have done a thousand other good Russians would have done."

She looked into his eyes as she said the last words. And then quickly, without waiting for his answer, she threw her arms about him and kissed him on both cheeks, even as he kissed her on both cheeks in the typical Russian fashion. They shook hands again. She took the reins of the horses in her hands and drove off at a fast clip, while he returned to the group of people assembled in the building that had once been an inn.

"Men," he cried out, "is it possible that there is not a single drop of drink amongst you?"

"It is against the law," they said.

"But you cannot see a man's heart being broken like this without trying to strengthen him," he answered. "Is there not a single

Russian amongst you whose heart beats like the heart of a Russian? Is there not a drop of vodka? Come, men, brothers, Russians."

He checked himself immediately, for he knew that once launched he would have gone on talking in the very opposite vein from what he had talked only a few minutes before; on the futility and the stupidity of their side, which had just appeared again clearly to him. Why not drink? It was the best thing. It was the Russian thing to do. Happiness? Bah—*nitchevo*.

But they laughed. "How that man is carrying on just because his wife has left him," they laughed. "Young people still love their women, revolution or no revolution," and they slapped him on the shoulders.

And some of the older men spoke good-naturedly and said, "Stay with us. And if she doesn't return by the appointed time, you'll find many a maiden willing to marry such a man as you. And it is easy to marry now; the easiest thing in the world. When you no longer care for a woman it is just as easy to get rid of her. And even the women themselves get rid of the men they no longer like. Why, you can't lay your hands on one of them. Just try to use a whip on one of them!

Just raise your voice against one of them, and you'll find out what it means to live in new Russia. But you needn't carry on so just because a wife has left you. She is beautiful. She is young and has a distinguished air. But they will think you are a counter-revolutionist to love a wife so!"

"Are you going to stay with us or are you going to go back home, my son?" a man who had till now kept quiet asked Ivan. "For if you are going to stay with us for a little while I ask you to be my guest."

His eyes twinkled as he spoke.

"I am going to rest for a while, and since you have been the first to ask me, I am only too willing to accept your hospitality," he replied.

And he made off with him immediately.

When Ivan arrived at the man's hut he disappeared into an adjoining room for a few minutes, and emerged soon, after closing the doors and the shutters of the square little window, with a bottle of vodka and a piece of black bread and a hunk of meat.

"It is against the law," he said, "but you need a drink, friend. What are laws to Russians, hein? Nitchevo."

CHAPTER VIII

Mariusha's people, angry and despairing because they had lost their horses with which Ivan had run away, ran into the palace, where they began to repay themselves for their losses. What they could not take in their packs and upon their shoulders they broke and smashed. But they found enough to repay them tenfold for the missing horses. And when the pillaging and wreaking instinct was fully awakened they no longer knew what they did. . . .

Mariusha would not leave the place when they finally decided to go. But her people were so anxious to get away with all the loot that they left her there, fully convinced that she was to follow them soon. Then the peasants began to fumble in the cellars and closets and look for more drink, breaking in doors and locks, even after the kniaz whom they led before them had shown them where everything was kept.

It was a long, drunken orgy, which wound up early in the morning with the kniaz himself as drunk as the rest of them, for he had somehow succeeded in getting back into their graces, as a Russian. They were now complaining together of all that had happened and all that was going to happen. The peasants forgot all the insults and injuries that they had heaped upon their lord, forgetting even that they had intended to kill him. They were hugging him and calling him tavarish. Yes, they were going to make him the staroste of the village, that he should lead them straight and interpret for them the new law. In the morning they were going to run after his daughter and the traitor who had saved her instead of killing her, and the kniaz should judge them.

But in the morning two people had taken hold of the befuddled mob, Mariusha and that man who had first denounced the kniaz for having whipped his father to death. They had somehow kept more sober than the rest. Mariusha had probably kept sober altogether, for the rage that was within her was much greater than the excitement she could have gotten out of the bottle. It was burning hot. No amount of drink could have extinguished her anger. And anyway she never was known to drink or to enjoy drink. It had always had to be forced upon her. She had enough fire within her. She did not need it.

But what a different Mariusha she was from the one Ivan had seen when he first lusted after her! She was no longer a little girl whose bare legs and bare arms and half bare bosom tempted men on the road. She was a grown-up woman, a furious woman, a revengeful woman, a purposeful woman. She had grown to all that in a few weeks. She had heard enough of Feodor's speeches to have a patter with which to command the attention of the peasants. They looked upon her as some miraculous being, forgetting altogether her origin, forgetting even that she had been with me, forgetting even that she was a cursed gypsy woman in whom nobody ever had much confidence. No man could have grown so fast as that girl had grown. Woman awakens from a long sleep when her passions are aroused. It is as if a hundred doors were suddenly torn open by one key.

And there was this Stephan, this man she had inveigled with her,—an ugly, cruel, stupid brute who was ready to do her bidding. She twisted him around her little finger any way she chose. She had made a slave of him in

THE VOLGA BOATMAN 93

a few hours. She told him who and what he was. He was going to be ruling Russia. She would make him the ruler of Russia. The two of them took complete command of the situation. They talked from the steps of the palace. They talked from upturned tables. They talked from the rears of carts.

Meanwhile the peasants felt very much in plenty, finding more and more drink and more and more food in the cellars of the palace, saturating themselves, drinking themselves to fury, whipped into obedience by these two adventurers, the only ones who had kept their heads and knew what they were doing.

Before the evening the peasants had dragged out all the things of the palace, emptied them in the middle of the yard and applied the torch to them; not before they had ripped and broken and smashed with their axes everything that was brought out.

Meanwhile Feodor's body was still lying where it had fallen; forgotten, trampled upon, knocked this way and that. It was only the following morning that Mariusha, to think of something new, to keep the peasants in excitement, thought of what to do with the dead body.

They dragged it out and carried the dead

one with great pomp through the roads and streets of several villages, carrying banners and flags on which they inscribed how Feodor had died, a martyr to the cause of the peasants, killed by the aristocracy. By order of Stephan they had tied the kniaz's hands with ropes behind his back, and compelled him to walk behind the cart which carried Feodor's body. Stephan and Mariusha were talking at every corner to the peasants who came up to inquire who the man was, whenever the funeral cart stood still.

People, idle as they were, deserted their hearths and their houses and followed the funeral cart. In a few hours the cortege was miles long, those at the end never knowing where the ones at the beginning were, winding in and out and stopping at crossroads before the wooden images of Christ and the Virgin.

They walked behind the dead body the whole day, and returned only late in the evening to their own village, where they buried Feodor in great haste in a shallow grave, for they were all too tired from so much walking and all still under the influence of drink. They only remembered what it was all about when they returned to the kniaz's yard in front

A Cecil B. De Mille Production. *The Volga Boatman.*
PRINCE NIKITA IS COMPELLED TO WATCH THE REVOLUTIONISTS GLUT THEMSELVES ON HIS LAVISH FARE.

of the former palace. In their stupid haste and carelessness they forgot to put up over Feodor's grave a sign, a cross, or anything which should mark Feodor's grave for those who wanted to know where he lay.

And now they began to talk about distribution, of how to distribute whatever had remained in the cellars, and the silver and the gold loot. But Stephan, in agreement with Mariusha, declared that they first had to dispose of the kniaz. And Kniaz Nikita, so tortured and so tired, so humbled, assented to that. He did not care what was happening, but life as it was was almost unendurable to him. He begged them as a brother, as a Russian, crying before them as if he was pleading for somebody else, that they should make an end of his miseries. He had been spat upon. He had been beaten. They had torn the clothes off his back.

But the peasants were slow in deciding, in spite of Stephan's urging them to do away with him. There was not a hand willing to take the death of the kniaz upon itself. Some, now, because they had again some sort of pity for him, and others because they were afraid of what might happen if the people of his kind should return to power. One never knew what could happen in Russia. And they knew that thousands of the most cruel deaths would not be enough to pay for the one life taken.

They were slow in deciding, and they temporized. The kniaz could not run away, the way they watched him, they argued. And since he could not run away, why not wait until they had decided amongst themselves and found out the best means?

Yet Stephan and Mariusha insisted. They improvised some sort of a tribunal in the big hall where they had banqueted only a few days before. And there, with Stephan and Mariusha acting as prosecuting attorneys, they judged the man not only for the sins he himself had committed, but for the sins his father and grandfather and many generations before him; and even for Ivan's own "treachery," as they called it, and his daughter's running away.

Even while they sat in so-called judgment they gorged themselves with drink, the bottles passing from one to the other. The kniaz sat and listened to all they said with bowed head. Too tired to understand what was happening, too anxious to have it all come to an end, too miserable to want to oppose them or to discuss with them, and yet too proud to ask for mercy from a horde of drunken people. He felt the pride of martyrs. His suffering had gone beyond physical pain. His body was numb.

Of course what they all said was right. The kniaz's father before him, and he himself, had been very cruel to the people. But was it right that they should judge one man for the sins of his father and his grandfather? Then Stephan, together with Mariusha, without many preambles, pronounced him guilty and in the same breath condemned him to death. And before anybody had turned around to know what had happened the execution had been carried out by Stephan's own hand. And after that the palace itself went up in flames, while Mariusha sang and danced to the drunken people.

The news of what had happened to the kniaz spread rapidly to the adjoining villages, and the example of it was so infectious that many other villages who had temporized with their former oppressors and landlords now took dire vengeance upon them. Stephan and Mariusha, after they had done their work in that village, became sort of traveling prosecutors, being called everywhere. With the rage of a bloodthirsty monster, Stephan left in his path corpses and ashes, acting as prosecuting attorney, as judge, and as executioner almost in every instance, with Mariusha getting wilder and wilder, and yet inquiring everywhere whether Ivan and Vera had not been seen. She traveled now along with Stephan as his wife. She had adorned herself with silks, and had her pockets stuffed with many jewels that she had looted here and there, and which she did not dare hang about her person. She dominated Stephan completely, for whenever his heart weakened or whenever his argument slackened, she supplied whatever was necessary, repeating one of the speeches of Ivan or of Feodor, and adding to it all the brutality, all the gross stupidity and cruelty which she knew would be effective with the people she talked to. Their salvation was in murder, in brutality, in destruction.

CHAPTER IX

MEANWHILE some order began to be established in the land. Like a hand extending itself from a great distance, it stretched itself slowly and covered and remained just long enough to put some order into the things. When all the drink had been lapped up and there was none other to be gotten, people began to feel that they could not live eternally on the loot near at hand. They suddenly discovered that though they had divided the land amongst themselves they had neither oxen nor horses to cultivate it with; and above all, that they did not have seed enough to cover one-tenth of the land that they possessed. And when the cry for seeds and working tools and oxen went up, the souls calmed down. They needed food for the land. Russia could not live on internal loot. Mouths could not be fed with words from orators.

But both Mariusha and Stephan had by this time won for themselves a considerable part in some branch of the government. They were valuable people. When nothing else could be done to keep the peasants in hand traitors could always be discovered and gotten rid of. And Mariusha and Stephan were both dramatic and romantic enough to distract and take away the mind of the people from what it had been dwelling upon.

And everywhere, going from village to village with Stephan, Mariusha was inquiring about Ivan's whereabouts, and about that of Vera; for she was absolutely certain that the two should be found together. The whole government was soon set upon the two, as if its life and existence depended upon their discovery. And Ivan, together with Feodor, had started all this.

After Ivan had implanted himself rather securely in the village of Mielnitz he thought it was much better policy to remain where he was instead of traveling around and being questioned by every one on the road. The tcheka was searching for him and Vera. There was no good in being anywhere as a stranger. He had neither passport nor papers, and was much more willing to stay among the strangers he was with than continue on the road. They sympathized with him because they had seen his "wife" go to see her parents, and believed everything he told them, including the tale that he was anxiously awaiting her return.

Meanwhile winter descended upon the land. The snow buried deep all the roads and huts, and most people closed themselves in within their habitations like bears going into winter quarters. Ivan remained to live with the old man who had first befriended him, who had given him that glass of vodka.

The long speeches were forgotten as soon as the snow had settled down. There was the same old hunger awaiting the people as in the times of the Czar. The words peasants and commissars had spoken had been empty wind which had not filled the provision bags, which people in Russia should lay up for the long winter months. There was hope that the government would come to help. But from where and how? The word "government" seemed to be an all-potent word for the peasants. It was their government! Why should it not come to fill their mouths, cover their backs, and heat their stoves? As if the government could order wheat and barley and corn to grow in the air above the clouds— wheat and barley and corn that had never been sown, never been harvested, and never threshed.

So they began to mutter against the soviet government. Why! They said it was in no way different from the former government. Why had they been talking so loud? It was an even worse government, for the other government, when they had raised a large enough cry, had occasionally sent down a few bags of corn. And now as the winter advanced they were not so sure that this government would be able to send them enough for seeds in the spring. And there was not a single grain of corn or wheat or barley to be had anywhere.

The peasants slaughtered their oxen and their cows, which would have died anyhow, for there was no feed for them.

It was the first long hunger Ivan had ever suffered. And many a time the people he lived with, and other people gathering together in the village hall, looked to him that he should help. He was afraid lest they tear him to pieces, like cannibals, seeing how hungry they were.

"Why don't you, Ivan, go and talk to the government? You can talk in a way we cannot. Go and tell them that we are all dying here. You spoke for the government. You are like one of theirs."

But they only spoke that way. They knew that there was no possible way by which he could, during those terrible storms, reach the seat of government. And he knew that even if he could get there he was in no way certain he could get them what they desired. Ivan thought of setting out on foot against all odds, but he hesitated against the prospect of dying on the way of hunger, of fatigue, or being eaten up by the wolves which prowled about in broad daylight in the middle of villages.

Then one day he saw Mariusha's gypsy tribe again. There they were, all, minus Mariusha, with well-fed horses. And they all looked well fed and well taken care of. They came in their sleighs, dropping in at what had formerly been the inn, and which was now the town's meeting place, and cried and begged and whined that they should be allowed to stay there for a few days. They begged food and drink while Ivan could see that their horses had been well fed by the smoothness and the luster of their coats.

He kept at a distance from the gypsies. He did not want to be recognized. He scented something was up, that they were looking for him. He expected them to tell the tale of how their daughter had been stolen. But they never said a word on the subject. Ivan's face was bearded now, and he kept his shapka well over his eyes, and to make the deception more complete limped on the right foot, and raised one shoulder higher than the other whenever he felt eyes resting upon him.

A day later Ivan heard them inquire very carefully and deftly whether a young gypsy woman, so and so, and they described her minutely, had been seen in the neighborhood. And then he knew that they had probably left their "pateran" on the road for Mariusha to follow them; and he knew that if she did feel inclined to do so, she could find out their whereabouts with ease and join them.

"It is a great pity," Ivan's host said to him when they returned home that night, "to see these poor travelers starving on the road. It is a great pity. It is a sin that good Christians should not be able to feed them and take care of them until they should be able to go further."

"There will be food in your hut to-night, but not for them," Ivan answered.

"From where? There is not a handful of anything in my house. And eating frozen meat of starved oxen without salt and without anything else has made me so sick I cannot think of food without a revulsion in my stomach. Oh, how I wish I had something else but dried meat!" he cried. "But from where and how? From where will you get food for us?" the old man questioned, thinking Ivan had gone insane suddenly.

Ivan smiled to himself, for he knew what he knew. He had learned from his former sojourn with the gypsies how they kept their food hidden in a double bottom of their cart; and how they kept everything precious hidden there. That night he left the old man in front of his door and went stealthily to the town house. Tunneling his way under the snow from quite a distance from where the sleigh had been left under a shed, Ivan burrowed until he was underneath it, and filled a bag with most precious and nourishing food, which he dragged back to his hut. He left, however, half of the food secreted outside, and after they had eaten their fill, he made sure that some of it remained for the days to come. Ivan slipped outside, threw the rest of the provisions upon his shoulder and returned to the sled. Before anybody knew what had happened he had again made away with the sleigh and the horses the gypsies had left outside, while they rested and cried starvation within the town hall.

CHAPTER X

AFTER Ivan left Vera with the reins in her hand, driving the horses, she drove first straight on before her in the direction the people had indicated to her. There was a long stretch of miles and miles, a sort of no man's land over which neither the bolsheviki nor the White forces ruled. And the peasants of this part of the country, obeying no rule and obeying both rules, scarcely dared to put their heads out of their huts. They had been raided and expropriated, which meant that their food and all provisions whatever had been taken away, first by the Red soldiers in a friendly way, and then by the White forces, who accused them that they had willingly given food to the enemy forces. They had been raided and despoiled and robbed in a friendly and in an unfriendly way by the Whites and the Bolsheviki. And such things happened several times to these people until they were left with nothing but the bones of their bodies and the skin over them, gaunt, parched, their eyes dry and glassy, of the

THE VOLGA BOATMAN

same color as the skin. It seemed as if even their finger nails were soon to be taken away, for these were the only things left to them with which they could scratch the earth should the time come when they should again plow and plant.

And when next spring did come, it was a great pity to see them look out into the fields, broad and rolling land that had at other times produced wheat, lying idle, getting hard just because of the lack of plows and beasts and seed. What had been forests once were all denuded. The trees were standing up, sickly, with only a little foliage on the top branches. Both beast and man had pulled off the bark for food.

And so Vera rode on through this desolate field that had been laid waste by people of her side and of the other side, laid waste by the long war that had preceded the revolution, in which so many of her people had been slaughtered. And suddenly as she was driving on, from behind a clump of trees a group of men, armed to the teeth, jumped out and stopped her horses.

"From where do you come and where are you going?" they called to her, holding the heads of the horses.

And when she had told them who she was, for she knew now that she was amongst people of her own side, they smiled with incredulity. They could not believe that Kniaz Nikita's daughter could be dressed as she was. They looked at one another understandingly, and one of them asked her again whether she was certain that she was who she said she was. For if she were not, he assured her that nothing but flaying her alive would satisfy Dmitri Ivanof.

Vera shuddered at the mention of the name. For it was Dmitri Ivanof to whom she had been engaged. And it was Dmitri Ivanof who had pulled the fatal trigger that had laid Feodor low to the ground. She had never been able to understand how he had brought himself to do that. He was a nice, quiet, young man who had been educated abroad, from whom everything Russian seemed to have been educated out. He never even spoke Russian, using French instead, as most Russian aristocrats were in the habit of doing. She had not been able to understand how he, so quiet and so sentimental, who played the piano so beautifully and sang with such a melodious voice, who looked so feminine in spite of his long silken blond mustache and dark blue eyes, how he could have brought himself to pull the trigger that killed a man. Of course he had done it in the heat of anger, and not from any inner conviction or deliberation that such a thing had to be done for some higher spiritual or patriotic reason.

"Dmitri Ivanof is here?" she asked of the man who had spoken to her. "Dmitri Ivanof? Lead me straight to him."

The men jumped in the cart and one of them relieved her of the reins. He conversed with her on the way. He meant to be friendly and chat with her, apparently, but in reality it was to ask her a thousand questions the answers of which he would furnish his superiors. And she knew from the questions he asked that he was no peasant but some *mestchanin,* some petty bourgeois, probably the son of a merchant, who had gone to school, a university man, most probably, in spite of his endeavor to talk the Russian of peasants.

They drove on for several hours, through tortuous roads and through paths in the forest before they arrived at a sheltered valley in which an army had been bivouacked, camping.

Sentinels had stopped them all along the way several times and they had had to identify themselves to them. And every time the man sitting near her had pronounced the name of Dmitri Ivanof, "This lady wants to see Dmitri Ivanof," the men would step aside for them, respect and terror in their eyes as they heard the name of Dmitri Ivanof repeated.

Soon after they arrived in the valley the men with her asked her to step down. The horse and wagon were led away. Two of the men placed themselves in front of her, three in the back, with bayonets fixed to their guns, and they led her on between huts and tents until they arrived at what had formerly been a large house but which had been partly destroyed. Meanwhile the other soldiers had assembled and walked next to the capturers of Vera at a distance, wondering what was going to happen. The White army was bivouacked in a destroyed village of large size.

A sergeant came out and asked the soldiers, after the usual military salute, where they had found this lady.

"She says," the leader of them explained, "that she is the daughter of Kniaz Nikita and that she wants to see Kniaz Dmitri Ivanof."

"Have you searched her?" was the question asked by the sergeant.

And at their answer that they had not he grew furious at such negligence, and pro-

THE VOLGA BOATMAN

ceeded to search her himself by feeling her body all over and wondering even after that operation was through whether he should not investigate further. Then he spoke in an impersonal way, without even looking at Vera.

"She may be Kniaz Nikita's daughter after all. How am I to know? But duty is duty, and you should have searched her before bringing her here. You shall be punished for that."

And then talking to Vera he said, "One day something terrible happened because we had not searched a prisoner. So you will pardon me if you are Kniaz Nikita's daughter."

Vera shrugged her shoulders.

"But where is Dmitri Ivanof?" she asked.

The soldiers looked at her questioningly and wondered whether they should listen to the strange woman and disturb the great man.

While all this was going on more idle soldiers assembled around Vera, until there were hundreds loitering, leaning against one another, pointing at her. The sergeant disappeared for a few moments, a bugle was blown, and presently Dmitri Ivanof jumped down from a horse in the midst of the crowd.

"Vera!" he cried out.

And when the soldiers had seen that he had

really recognized her, that she was who she said she was, they scattered and disappeared, none of them wanting to be recognized as the one who had so undignifiedly treated her. How much like old Russia, Vera could not help thinking.

But she had another look at Dmitri. He was a Dmitri she had not known before. There was something harsh and cruel about his mouth and his eyes. There was something terrible about him. It frightened her to think he was spoken of with such great fear by the soldiers who scampered away at his approach.

"How did you get here?" he finally asked.

"That is a long story," she answered.

And she felt all at once far more restraint with him than she had felt with the soldiers who had captured her.

"I suppose you know," he said, after they had gotten into the house, "that we have avenged the death of your father."

"Avenged the death of my father! Avenged the death of my father!" she cried out. "When? How?"

"A hundred people have paid with their lives for his death. And we have razed the village to the ground."

She was dumbfounded to hear the news.

THE VOLGA BOATMAN

"How could you?" Vera cried. "How could you do that?"

"It was to avenge the kniaz, and also to set an example," he answered.

"But how have you come to rule all these people? I did not know that you had even been in the army."

She broke down and wept bitterly, for she had not even known that her father had been killed. In reality one of the motives she had had in running towards the White forces was to ask them to go and help her father and rescue him. And now that she found that his death had already been avenged, she felt bitter towards the avengers.

CHAPTER XI

DMITRI was a suave, soft, feminine, piano-playing, foreign-educated, young man whom Vera had never thought capable of killing even a fly. There are many like Dmitri in Russia. Their fathers and grandfathers had married foreign women. And many have inherited all the superficial qualities of their mothers, by whom they were pampered and educated. But they have also inherited all the barbarism of the old ancestors of their fathers, all the savagery of the Tartar and Cossack blood. And Russians are able to display themselves in both colors. And the worst of all their traits always comes to the surface.

While in peace time, abroad, or among cultured people, they are refined gentlemen, with most artistic tendencies. At lovemaking they are ready with lute and song. In music they love only the finest, the tenderest. But when they are drunk, or when their blood is otherwise stirred, all the savagery of their ancestors comes to the fore, with even greater intensity than if they were pure-blooded Tartars. And then their cruelty knows no bounds. Tigers, hyenas, serpents, a mixture of the three, that is what such Russians are. The Russian nobility is the mongrel of all races.

It was this mongrel blood that had first spoken when Dmitri had pulled the trigger that killed Feodor. It did not matter to him that he endangered the others, his own fiancée, her father. He shot. He killed. Nothing mattered. *Nitchevo.* And it was this savagery and intensity which helped him ride through a thousand dangers until he had met with the White forces which he joined. Dmitri was striving to reinstate the old Russian aristocracy on the shoulders of the Russian people.

There were many of his comrades, school and university comrades, who were high officers in that army. Too young to go to the war, he had been kept at home, but he was a soldier, Dmitri. He had been destined for the army by his parents.

Within a short time he became the active military prosecutor; the judge of spies and people from whom they wanted information as to the movements of the Red army, or of people whose sympathies they suspected. There was a terror, a White terror, instituted to oppose the Red terror then working in the land. The first thing that was installed when a town was captured by the White army was a tribunal. Dmitri became the head of that so-called military justice. His name became one of the most feared names in the country; people trembled when it was mentioned. He used his mind to invent horrible tortures in order to extract information and admissions from people. There was neither quarter nor pity in the hands that played the piano so delicately. The hands that plucked the strings of the guitar with such gusto were also the hands that strangled many a man, the hands that stabbed and tortured many a woman, in the interests of "his" people, or in the stupid lust that had been aroused within him. It was partly the terror which he had created that had made it possible for the White army to advance as far as it had, menacing so strongly the rule of the Reds. For a while it seemed it was only a question of time before the Whites, helped as they were clandestinely by foreign powers, would again seize the reins of the country and rule Russia. It was terror and cruelty, and not feat of arms that won for them many a victory over the Reds.

* * * * *

And Dmitri sat down near Vera to explain the White army. To explain not his cruelty but to explain how they were soon to reconquer Russia again, to take it away from the rabble and the foreigners who had taken possession of it.

And even as he spoke Vera felt that it was not love of the people that made him speak so eloquently, but only the reëstablishment of the old rulership. There was no question in his mind as to whether the White forces or the Bolshevik forces were the better ones suited to rule Russia for the better existence of the Russian people. It was just the despoiler's instinct that drove him on, that drove all of them on.

She saw things in a different light. She was not certain that the Reds were right. She was not certain that the Whites were right. Yet . . . she belonged socially to the Whites.

But above all these considerations was the anguish for the death of her father. She partly accused Dmitri for having been guilty of his death, and partly accused herself for having permitted Ivan to run away with her and leave the old man behind.

And yet all this had to be forgotten. There was no remedy for it. What had been done had been done. And she knew that from then on she would have to cope with Dmitri, who would insist on marrying her. She loathed him now. She smelled the moist, fetid odor of the blood of his victims about him. Even before she had known the cruelties he had committed she could read this in his eyes. His delicate white hands seemed to her to be clammy with the blood of people whom he had murdered or had had murdered.

A hundred people of her own village had paid with their lives for the death of her father. He had spoken of their death without a tremor. She wondered who was murdered. She knew almost every one of the village. Could it have been George or Nikolai? Anton or Leo? Vladimir or Gregory? These were people she had met every day. People to whom she had talked. Whose children she knew. Whose wives she knew. People she had consoled when they were bereaved of dear ones. People whom she had nursed through illnesses. People to whom she had brought bread in days of famine. And they

THE VOLGA BOATMAN

had been killed to no purpose. And the huts in which these people had lived had been destroyed, razed to the ground. Dmitri had told her the story.

And as he told her the story he gloried in it. As if the shooting of these poor people compensated for the blood of her father! He, Dmitri, who had pulled the trigger to kill that man, the man who could not have been but a gentle soul from the way he spoke—that Feodor, that stranger.

* * * * *

Dmitri watched her as she sat quietly and mused, and he noticed how she withdrew every time he attempted to come nearer to her. He had meanwhile given orders that temporary lodging be prepared for her until he could find suitable quarters. They were an army, he told her, and there were few ladies about except a certain kind of women who still trailed after regiments.

After he had whispered to one of the men, food was served on expensive trays.

"You must eat now, Vera. You must be very hungry," he told her, and then sat down by her side.

She was hungry, and so she ate while he talked on and on.

"But now," she said, when she had finished the last morsel, "what are you going to do now?"

"Within two weeks we shall have taken possession of Moscow. We shall rule Russia again. Two weeks later five or six thousand men will swing from five or six thousand gibbets from one end of Russia to the other, to teach a lesson to those who might attempt another coup like the one that deposed our Czar. Five or six thousand will swing from gibbets, and they will hang there for a month so that every one should see and learn the lesson. There are many other things, Vera, that we shall do. There won't be a Jew left alive in Russia. We shall flay them before we drown them like rats in the rivers."

"And what after?" Vera asked, more and more horrified.

"After," and his face beamed and smiled. "Why after it will be as before," and he edged closer to her. "I shall marry you, Vera."

And he began making love as tenderly as any refined gentleman. He recited poetry. His eyes covered themselves with a moist film. His voice was soft and musical. And he spoke French again.

Vera held him off with her eyes. When he

left her a while later, because he was called away, she shuddered at the thought that if not for the things that had happened she would have married him and borne children from him, without even a glimpse into his real soul.

She had seen cruelties before in her life, when muzhik peasants had beaten their women pitilessly. She had seen cruelties, when her father, or some other one of his entourage, would beat a muzhik because he had turned up drunk to work or had stolen something.

These were uncouth people, and their cruelties were frequently inflictions of pain to correct an imaginary wrong or a real wrong, or because of fury. But this elegant and effeminate Dmitri Ivanof was so refined, he would think of entirely different cruelties. She imagined him sitting down alone and inventing cruelties, refined punishments or tortures, planning and scheming how to make the torture last longer and be more terrible, developing a technique of torture, in keeping with his degree of intelligence. She remembered now how he had frequently told her he did not love folk songs because they were much too simple. They had had many dissentions on this subject. He loved intricate and difficult music: Wagner and Debussy, Ravel and Strauss. His cruelties and tortures were probably as refined as the music he loved. He would forget in the development of the technique of these cruelties even the aim at which they were pointed. More like a spider than a human being he stretched out his invisible net in the light of the sun to catch the unwary, the innocents.

She had not mused long when he returned to sit down near her.

"I have given orders to place you comfortably," he informed her.

He edged and hovered about her, trying to make her feel at ease, covering her with a thousand little niceties and attentions. Before long he accompanied her to a tent not far from his, very comfortably furnished with things that had been pilfered from residences of the wealthy. Though she was very tired, she could not fall asleep. She passed a white night. The outside noises frightened her; making her jump up in her cot, sitting up ready to meet any emergency.

Early the following morning there was much hubbub and noise in the camp. It was only then that she realized how enormous the camp was. Several women came to be intro-

THE VOLGA BOATMAN

duced to her. And from them she learned that there were hundreds of them, wives and sisters and daughters of the men who had fled before the onrush of the revolution and who had banded together now under the leadership of a group of men. Dmitri Ivanof was one of the heads. They had high hopes of soon taking over the power from the bolsheviki and putting themselves at the head of a new government, the Denikin forces.

And these people were also divided, the women especially, in two groups. There were those who urged moderation when they should come into power. The peasants were no longer to be treated as slaves and beasts of burden. The day of absolute despotism which had ruled Russia was gone, they argued. More democracy had to be ushered in to make of Russia a country like other civilized countries.

And there was another group who urged the very contrary. It was because there had been too much liberalism in Russia in late years, they argued, that what had happened had happened. Should they come into power again the liberalism would be wiped out; all the liberties that the peasants enjoyed would be taken away from them. Russia needed another Peter the Great, or an Ivan Grosnik, a ruler of whom all the peasantry should be afraid and tremble. Only such a ruler could keep Holy Russia intact.

And when Vera argued for even more democracy than the first group had argued, they all turned against her. Had she been scared just because a few peasants had risen against the aristocracy? Just because a few stupid beasts of burden had brayed louder than they had brayed before? Why, the whole world was with them, the aristocrats of Russia, and was willing to help them establish the absolute government that they had had before.

If she cared to know more details about that, let her ask Dmitri Ivanof. He knew. There was no other way of putting down the revolution than by drowning it in blood. In another few days, when their army would be ready, they were to push forward and conquer village after village, hamlet after hamlet, town after town, until they had reconquered the seat of government. Arms were being sent to their help. Ammunition was arriving from everywhere. Food, stores, uniforms, weapons, artillery, all were on the way. France had to come to their help because the old government owed France so much money, which the new government had absolutely refused to pay. England knew that if the new government remained for any length of time, all that they had invested in Russia would be lost. And it had been a wise policy, owing these countries money; a wiser policy even than making treaties with them. There was no wiser policy than owing to strong governments money. One was sure that in time of need they would come to help in order to get back what was owed them. There was an army in the north. Kolchak, the Czechs, the former prisoners beating their way from Siberia were with them. Victory could not help being on their side.

CHAPTER XII

DURING the next few days Dmitri Ivanof showed himself very seldom to Vera. She had just fleeting glimpses of him as he rode past her tent and inquired about her health and comfort. But she knew from the little conversation she had with him that the other women had imparted to him her views, her attitude. He made only slight allusions to them, but it was to make her understand that he knew what she thought.

A sudden realization that she was more a prisoner than a guest dawned upon her. She felt herself watched by both the men and the women who circled around her. She felt herself spied upon. And the women no longer talked to her freely about their own thoughts, but let her talk, to draw her out. And she knew that everything she said was being memorized and discussed and analyzed.

And one of the women plied her several times with questions as to the details of her escape. How had it happened? And how did the man look who had saved her? And

A Cecil B. De Mille Production.   *The Volga Boatman.*
HAVING OVERPOWERED THE SENTRY, THE REVOLUTIONISTS PREPARE TO ATTACK THE ARISTOCRATS.

what was it that made him save her? they inquired. And then they wanted to know exactly the route she had taken and where they had stopped together. And where did she think the man was now? Did she think that he had gone further up north to join the bolsheviki? Or did she think that he had remained in the same village with the people? She refused to tell them the exact route for fear of betraying Ivan to them. He was on the other side, true, but he had saved her life.

And one of them, a German wife of a Russian high officer, put a warm arm around her waist, drawing her to her, and asking in an intense voice, "But, dearest, I am sure you must have fallen in love with him, seeing that he was such a hero. And it is not impossible that you have made a rendezvous with him, in case you should ever want to see him again. Where, where will you meet him? Oh, what a man he must be!"

Vera looked at her with disgust. She was certain the woman had been sent to her by Dmitri Ivanof, who wanted to know why she had not received him with greater enthusiasm, why she had not been readier in her acceptance of him.

Meanwhile the activity in the camp increased. Ammunition and artillery and stores of food and clothing arrived from somewhere. Soldiers were being drilled daily. Cossacks arrived from everywhere on their horses, and were getting back into the old battle spirit. Clarions sounded, battalions were formed. Officers in foreign uniforms were drilling the men who manipulated machine guns and heavier artillery. It had at first seemed to Vera to be only a small camp composed of a few thousand people. But she soon realized that the camp was much bigger than she at first thought it was, and it augmented daily.

Dmitri Ivanof came to see her. He had been riding together with a small group of higher ranked officers.

"I am going away for a few days," he said to her. "But you shall be taken care of as well as if I were here. And if God will be good to us, one of the first things we shall do will be to rebuild your ancestral palace that has been razed, and make it an even more beautiful place than it was. And remember that."

He was gone before she had said a word.

A few hours after cannons began to boom in the distance. They boomed for several hours. And then there was a sudden silence, and large groups of cavalry passed by her tent at high speed. More villages had been razed. The anti-revolutionary army advanced towards Moscow.

That night the camp moved forward, leaving detachments behind to occupy what was already held. The following day the very village in which Ivan had stayed and from which Vera had gone to rejoin Dmitri Ivanof and his kind was occupied by the anti-revolutionary forces. The inn where they had first stopped, and which had become during the rule of the peasants a communal house, was one of the few houses that remained on its foundations. Only part of the roof had been torn away by a missile.

* * * * *

The third day two riders came to Vera. They asked her to join them immediately. Many other women were escorted likewise and were given place in that inn to live in. The old peasant who had taken Ivan to his home, and who had acted as his host, looked long at Vera from the depth of his small squinting eyes. He remembered that he had seen her not long before, and wondered under what circumstances, where and how.

Vera noticed him looking at her, and thinking that he had definitely recognized her she attempted to talk to him. But she was afraid. She was afraid that if she was seen talking to him the peasant would probably be questioned as to what the kniazine had said to him. And he might give away Ivan's whereabouts. Vera did not know that he had already departed and was far away.

And Dmitri Ivanof would want to know why she was anxious to know where Ivan was. That would be the question that would set Dmitri Ivanof on his ears. And if caught, she knew to what tortures Ivan would be submitted before being strung up.

And yet the peasant looked at her and looked at her without placing her. She wondered why he looked at her so intently.

Dmitri Ivanof came to see Vera to inquire how comfortable she was.

"My dear," he said, "I have ordered a search of the entire village. It shall begin at midnight. I am anxious to see what it will bring forth. Such searches, 'oblavas,' always fill me with excitement."

Vera trembled from head to foot at the sound of his words. And the same spirit that had made her dance at the sound of a Russian folk tune a few minutes before certain death, the same spirit now animated her. They were all Russians, all of them. Why were they torturing and killing each other? How much better it would be if they should go out and talk to them, convince them by word of mouth instead of trying to urge upon them their thoughts with cannon and lead.

"Dmitri Ivanof, why must you disturb the poor people at midnight? Why must you scare them and torture them? Is it not enough what you have done? These poor people are no more bolsheviki than they are anti-revolutionists. They are Russians. They have always been good and loyal and stupid Russians. Let us talk to them. Let your men go out to-morrow after daybreak and call them in front of the steps here, and let a few of us, myself if you so desire, talk to them. Let us tell them that we do not mean to destroy them, that we do not mean to treat them as enemies, that we want them to be our friends, that we want to bring back old Russia. That we want them to be happier than they are and that we believe that under a Czar they will be happier than they are. Let us promise them more than they have had till now. You will see that you can do a lot more in that way than in the way you are doing."

She talked to him long and entreatingly. She even allowed him to put his arm about her waist and press his head close to hers as she tried to convince him to do what she wanted him to do. But when he still remained adamant to her proposals she arose in great fury and swore that she would never let him come near her a single step, that she preferred to die rather than have anything to do with the enemy of her people. She told him he reeked blood; that he was a hideous monster.

At that he recoiled and looked at her squintingly, measuring her from head to foot, at first with an attitude of superiority and then with an attitude of pity.

"How little you know me," he said to her. "How very little you know me. Yet just because I do not want to disturb your sleep, knowing that you will be awake thinking that I may do harm to the muzhik, I am going to let them sleep if they can to-night. Maybe in the morning you will have thought better of it, and would no longer feel the way you do.

* * * * *

That morning Vera and the other women were awakened by the booming of cannon and by the bursting of shells in the middle of the village. But this time it was not the cannon and shells of their own side but from the cannon and shells of the Red army that was advancing against them.

The women and non-combatants were sent immediately to the rear, and in the move and hurry Vera had no glimpse of Dmitri Ivanof. Helter-skelter the non-combatants flew before the bursting shells that fell in the village, burying themselves in church and house and digging deep holes in the roads. And in this flight of the non-combatants to the rear the older men and women of the village, as well as the children and whatever little belongings they still had, were taken along. The younger element was hurriedly armed with whatever weapons were at hand and sent to the rear as part of the anti-revolutionary army.

For days and days the fighting at the front lasted. It zigzagged. There were times when the whole anti-revolutionary force moved ahead for miles and miles at a time, only suddenly to be compelled to move back again, with a continual augmenting of the non-combatants who joined the rear lines; weeping, crying and groaning, carrying heavy bundles upon their shoulders and children upon their necks—emaciated, starved beings who seemed to hold together miraculously and stand up only by the joints of their limbs, which somehow still kept the dead bodies erect.

The non-combatants in the rear, together with Vera, knew the way the battle went by the advance and retreat. It was as if children were playing on a gigantic seesaw. The whole day fresh soldiers seemed to pour in from the rear to the forward lines of the anti-revolutionary army, and the whole night this same army came back red, red with the blood of their wounds. Brother killing brother, father killing son, in this attempt to rule one another. That is Russia. That is what Russia has always been.

At the end of the fifth day the anti-revolutionary army had just advanced a little beyond the village which they had first occupied. And Vera knew in the continual action back and forth, and from the booming of the cannon at a distance, how the villages between the armies that seesawed back and forth had been destroyed, how many innocents had been killed, how many churches had been blown up in the air, what devastation had taken place. They had razed down not only houses but whole forests in the attempt to cut down obstruction to forward and backward movement. She remembered one forest she had passed on her way to join the anti-revolutionary forces. It was now an immense heap of splintered wood, lying in the most fantastic manner, in high piles, one on top of the other.

As far as her eyes could see from the roof of the house in which she had been placed, there was nothing but devastation, nothing but ruin, with only the rain of bullets and shrapnel and the clouds of smoke bursting everywhere.

And then as if from nowhere a bullet whistled close by her, so close indeed she felt not only its whistling but also the heat of it as it passed her by.

She ducked and jumped down from the thatched roof, only to be again face to face with Dmitri Ivanof, who eyed her critically and asked why she had gone to the top of the roof. He had to know. She explained to him that she merely went up because of curiosity. But her answer did not satisfy him. He left her standing without any mark of politeness, shaking his head doubtfully. And Vera knew that from then on she would be observed even closer than she had been and she would be more a prisoner than ever. For already they referred to her as the Kniazine of Dmitri Ivanof.

CHAPTER XIII

THERE are people who have one way of doing things, one way of talking, one way of thinking, one way of walking. Life is only what is within them. And if the way they talk and the way they think and the way they walk does not happen to be the right way, it is not because of their fault but because of things outside them. They are right. The whole world is wrong.

And there are other people who have not any definite way of doing these things, who watch how life goes on outside them and then adapt themselves to the immediate needs, and adjust themselves to what they have to do or what they have to say. There are people who are so deliberately. And there are others who are so malleable that they fit into all these things without ever thinking how and why they do it.

Had things gone on in the old-fashioned way Stephan, Mariusha's new man, would have gone on in the old-fashioned way. He would perhaps have laid on the stick a little heavier on a horse or an ox. He would have kicked perhaps a little more violently the cow. And had he gotten married to one of the muzhik girls he would perhaps have beaten her a little more frequently than the other men used to beat their wives. There would not have been any great difference between him and the other people, except perhaps when drunk, when he would have wept louder than the others. He would have been guilty of little cruelties; little cruelties of the kind of which all Russians are guilty; if only for the occasion to chastise themselves a little stronger and to humble themselves a little more when the crisis has passed. But along came the revolution. Along came the great opportunity of being cruel to people who had been cruel to him and to his people for generations past. There was the murder of Feodor. Along came the opportunity to avenge himself on the kniaz. And the aftermath of it, the razing and the burning of the whole village by Dmitri Ivanof's hordes, from which raid Stephan, Mariusha and a few other people escaped alive.

And lo, Stephan's cruelty raised him several degrees above the other people. There was no intelligence needed, no love. No heart, no sentiment. No knowledge. And the man who was the cruelest, who had the heart to avenge himself in the swiftest and the most cruel way, rose above the other people. And because of his swift and cruel vengeance people began to look up to him and set him above themselves. In a short time he became a leader of the people and guided by him they went over into the bolshevik camp after his village had been isolated by the White soldiers. And the tales of his cruelties and vengeances spread by his band soon made for him a first place in the councils and at the meetings of the leaders. He was made a high commissar of justice. Dmitri Ivanof on the White side. Stephan on the Red.

And in that commissariat he had the able assistance of Mariusha. That slip of a girl had rapidly grown into a woman. Perhaps what actuated her was the desire to avenge herself on Ivan because he had left her; or the desire to avenge the death of Feodor, for whom she had conceived a great liking, and had hoped that she might in time pry herself loose from Ivan and go over to his friend. Feodor himself had conceived a great liking for her, and it was more because of her that he had decided to leave his wife and follow the road with them.

From the very first Mariusha knew how to be useful, not only to Stephan, whose wife she had become, but also to her own people; of whom hundreds, nay thousands, were wandering the roads, spying for one side and the other, intriguing with one side and the other, persecuted and shot by both one side and the other. Gypsies were both prey and hunters.

Amongst her own people she began to be known as queen. Through frequent meetings with her father and the rest of her tribe, she ruled over the vast thousands and thousands of gypsies that spread all over Russia. And theirs was a rich harvest from the revolution. Gold ikons from the churches. Silver candelabras. Old paintings. Jewels. Sacramental robes. Everything found its way to the bottom of carts and to secret hiding places, where these things were piled in large stores. And these things in time found their way across the border to be distributed and sold throughout all the world. Through Finland to Germany. Through the Scandinavian countries into France, from there to England and from there to America. A long chain of gypsies distributed these things all over the world, pearls, diamonds, necklaces, everything that could be robbed and taken from anywhere, from the houses of the former wealthy, from churches and homes which were plundered. It was taken out of Russia in carloads.

And yet this was only part of Mariusha's activity. Almost all gypsydom had been spread over the country as a net, and every one had a word portrait of Ivan's features, and every one was searching for him, and every one was ready to let Mariusha know as soon as they set their eyes upon him or Vera.

By the time she and Stephan had reached Moscow, high now in the councils of the bolsheviki, only very few people knew of her origin. She had so fully adapted herself to conditions, and her memory served her so well to repeat the speeches she had heard from Ivan and Feodor, and later from a lot of other people, that Stephan became a large figure mainly because of her ability, mainly because of her manners and airs.

There were a hundred legends about her. How in reality she was the daughter of a kniaz who had gone over to the bolsheviki; the daughter of an old aristocrat whose opin-

THE VOLGA BOATMAN

ions had always been very liberal, the kind of which there were many in old Russia.

From time to time Mariusha would be seen in flashing colors and flashing jewels. And there were also reports of great wealth that she still possessed. But this was spoken of kindly, in the manner of conceding to the former aristocrat some weakness.

Stephan and she were now living in one of the official houses. In some miraculous way, just as many other things happened at that time in Russia, this cruel, illiterate peasant became the animating spirit of the secret police. He became known not only through Russia but through the rest of the world as "Silent Stephan." From his desk orders were sent out that brought many a man and many a woman to his little room to be questioned. From this very same little office went out orders that sent bullets through the hearts of many people whose answers were not satisfactory to Stephan. Hundreds of people were thrown into jails to await their turn until the busy man should have time to question them. All the cruelties of all the inquisitions put together would hardly be more than the ABC of the tortures to which this man subjected his victims.

And many a day he acted both as prosecuting attorney, judge and executioner at one and the same time. When irritated by an unexpected answer or by an answer which he did not understand, he would rise from his chair as calmly as if he meant to go to light a cigarette, and plunge the dagger into the heart of the victim.

What a pair he and Dmitri Ivanof would have made! Two brothers in cruelty. One on the White side and one on the Red side.

Stephan's name and reputation spread all over the country to such a degree that the whole of Russia trembled at the mere mention of it. Those who worked under him thought that he was endowed with some supernatural power. They never could lie to him. His eyes were so searching it seemed to them that he looked through to the bottom of their very souls. Even his henchmen spoke in whispers about him, and never pronounced his name without first secretly or mentally crossing themselves. He always seemed to be near them whenever they talked about him.

And yet though he inspired such fear in everybody, to Mariusha he was nothing but a tool; for she knew exactly what he was worth and what animated him. And while the nets were continually spread all over Russia to get in all the counter-revolutionists and all those who were reported to conspire against the revolutionary government, in reality the net was spread merely to catch Ivan into it, and to enrich Mariusha's people. And every time that net, after being pulled in, failed to contain Ivan as one of the fish, Stephan passed a miserable quarter of an hour with Mariusha.

"What use is there to have as much power as you have, if you do not know what to do with it? All your men are betraying you. Perhaps that Dmitri Ivanof of whom you hear so much spoken is nobody else but Ivan, who is even now undermining your power! He is the greatest traitor of all of them. If it were not for him the whole of Russia would now be bolshevik. You would be at the head of all. You and I. And you because I have put you there. But your men are fools and traitors. And you . . . that," and she snapped her fingers at him.

And to her gypsies Mariusha would tell; "I shall take everything away from you. I shall have you all brought into Stephan's room and thrown into jails. What good are you if you cannot do one thing for me? You have become fat and lazy, and all your wits have left you."

Some one had told Mariusha's father that Ivan had been seen somewhere in Odessa. She sent word to her father that she wanted him to come immediately to see her. She gave him a bag of gold, and held another bag full of diamonds in the other hand as she spoke to him.

"You and the rest of you go to Odessa and bring Ivan with Vera, or Ivan alone, or Vera alone, either of the two or both to me. And I want either of them or both of them, alive here. Use all this bag of gold for that purpose. And if you bring them here, either of them or both of them, you shall have this bag of diamonds. But don't ever dare show your face without either of them. Now go and do that quickly."

Then she went to Stephan, and asked him to set his people to work in the same direction. She had worked upon the simpleton's mind in such a way that he believed that all of revolutionary Russia was endangered because of Ivan's being alive. He was firmly convinced that as long as he had not accomplished Ivan's capture the other things he did and all the other things that were being done in Russia were of no avail. As if Ivan were some monster who could do everything he wanted to do; while they, millions of them, could not accomplish anything against him.

Their information was correct. Ivan had been in Odessa for a very short while. He was sitting in one of the cafés one day waiting for a friend, when he noticed several gentlemen coming in. They watched Ivan from a distance, though they seemingly talked amongst themselves of current things.

When Ivan's friend arrived, who was an influential member of the revolutionary committee, a commissar in fact, he whispered to him:

"At the table opposite you, and probably watching you, are four members of the tcheka. There must be a mistake somewhere, Ivan, and I am just trying to think how to intervene so that you shall not have a bad half hour, or a bad half moon before the mistake has been corrected."

"But how do you know?" Ivan inquired.

"Oh, I know them," he answered.

And Ivan, knowing that he was in the high councils of the government, knew that what he told was true. He wondered whether there was any means of escape from the henchmen. He wondered whether his "betrayal," which he had so carefully covered up in the last months, had suddenly become known, and wondered how he could explain before a bullet had gone through his heart! For Russia had no time for justice's slow way. A suspected man was better dead than alive. And though he was himself one of the influential commissars, he knew that it would be a miracle if he could live through an explanation of any kind.

As he was thinking a group of swarthy gentlemen appeared in the same café. He had one look at them and knew that he had seen them elsewhere. And though they had shaven their beards and wore muzhiks' costumes he knew that he had seen the eyes of these people. And it instantly flashed through his mind that they were tzigans. Ivan raised his lids under the eyebrows to look at them closer, and recognized the two who were sitting facing him as people of Mariusha's tribe. They seemed unconcerned about Ivan, but he knew that their sudden appearance was because of him and wondered whether they were in league with the tcheka men.

He placed his hand in his pocket to make sure that the automatic revolver he always carried was there. He resolved to sell his life as dearly as possible. He had hardly decided that, while his friend sat near him seemingly unconcerned, yet planning how best to come to his help when it should become necessary, when the tcheka men, spreading from their table to different angles of the room, concentrated themselves upon Ivan's table. Four left hands placed themselves upon his shoulders, and four automatic pistols were placed at different parts of his body at one and the same time. And then one of them said:

"Life is sweet. It is better to die a little later than to die now. Don't you think so, tavarish? So it is better that you follow us instead quietly without attempting any disturbance."

Ivan's friend, who was known to them, gave them a signal and interfered.

"This must be a mistake. This must be a mistake. For he is one of ours, a friend of mine. I vouch for him personally."

"We have orders, tavarish," the leader of the four answered, "orders from the highest place. And we have answered for him with our lives. So if you care to come along and explain what you know, we shall be only too willing to let you accompany us. Indeed we ask you to come along with us, tavarish."

At that moment a dozen or more tzigans who had been sitting at different tables, seemingly occupied with themselves, jumped up to their feet; and led by Mariusha's father, they jumped upon the tcheka men in an attempt to take possession of Ivan.

There were several revolver shots fired and Ivan could hear in the noise the gurgles of several throats that had been cut. In the fight between the two factions who wanted to get possession of Ivan he was more or less left alone. And then his pistol spoke, and spoke to one who would never speak again.

Ivan crashed through the rear of the house, through kitchen and window, made use again of his gun, first against one set of people who had surrounded the place, and again against a swarthy group who watched from a distance the ones who had surrounded the house.

He ran as fast as his feet would carry him down to the Black Sea, where a wide row of white stone stairs descends to the water. He lay hidden under an upturned canoe for the rest of the night, listening to every noise, alarmed at the rumbling of the town.

In the morning Ivan heard that that particular coffee house in which he had been sitting had been burned to the ground, that several tcheka men had been killed by the secret agents of the Whites, who were there to protect one of their spies whose name was as yet not to be given to the public. Yet this much was told him. One of the men who had been trusted by the bolsheviki as one of their staunchest friends, nay, as one of the men in whom they laid great hopes, had suddenly been convicted as an enemy of the people, as a spy in the pay of foreign powers. Of course what they said was untrue, a tissue of lies.

He recognized in this description his poor friend. Ivan lay hidden there most of the day on the shore of the sea, wondering whether he should not deliberately give himself up in order to free him. But he knew how futile such a thing would be. He would not help him, and would only commit suicide.

Both Mariusha's people and the agents sent out by Stephan, those who were still alive, returned empty-handed. After listening to the report of Stephan's agents Mariusha, who sat near Stephan, bit her lips until they bled.

"What shall I do with them?" Stephan asked, turning around to Mariusha. "What shall I do with these fools? What shall I do with these fools?" Stephan asked again and again.

"Leave them to me," she answered.

"And what will you do with them?"

"There is an old dungeon down in this palace," Mariusha said. "I have seen it myself. Send them down there, and I shall attend to the rest."

A little later she received her father, who came weeping and crying, telling her how the enemies had come there to defend the traitor whom they had gone to catch. And the garbled story they told was that Ivan was guarded by hundreds of men and that they had had to fight against all of them and could not succeed.

And as he spoke, Mariusha's anger rose every second.

"And would you recognize the enemies, those who have hindered you from taking Ivan and bringing him here?" she asked her father and the other men of the tribe.

"Of course we would," her father and the other people answered.

"And what would you do to them, anything short of killing them, if I put them face to face with you, and put good harapniks into your hands?"

"We shall beat them until our hands are limp," the old man swore.

"Good, then," she said, "wait here until I return."

And then she asked that the tcheka men be brought to her from the dungeon.

"Would you recognize the people who have prevented you from bringing the traitor here?" she asked them.

"Of course we would, kniazine," they answered.

"And if I gave you good short knuts in your hands, would you know how to use them, short of killing them? But remember, I want no one dead!"

"Until our arms will hurt," they assured her, "if this would only clear us before Stephan Alexandroff."

"Very well," she said. "You go back into your dungeon, but with your clothes off. I have my reason for that. I want the clothes off you to make sure you are not going to run away. And I shall get your knuts ready."

A moment later she returned to her own people, including her father, and asked them to strip themselves naked.

"But why?" the old man asked. "Why should we do this?"

"I have a reason," she said, as she put

the harapniks, short-handled leather-thonged whips, in their hands.

And then she let them all together into a large, well-lit dungeon. Upon recognizing one another they fell upon one another like savages. Mariusha, who had bolted the doors from without, danced in glee and yelled with great pleasure at every loud shriek of pain that came from within. The fools! She was teaching them once forever how to obey orders.

The swishing of the whips and the slashing of flesh continued for a half hour. Then she sent for Stephan. And when she told him what was happening inside the room his face lit up in great joy, and standing outside he entreated and begged her that she should let him in. He wanted to witness what was taking place inside. He grinned and jeered and encouraged the people within.

"Now," he shrieked. "Show it to them! Give it to them, tavarish! Don't let the enemies hit you! Tavarish! Hit away at the enemy without any pity! Hey! One more, one more!"

When the beating inside had ceased Stephan and Mariusha opened the doors and went in. Two dozen naked bodies were lying on the wet ground, writhing in pain, covered with welts, their flesh torn, their eyes bleeding. There was not a single one who could do more than crawl on the ground, and still their hands held on to the knuts and the harapniks with which they had been sent in to dripple one another.

CHAPTER XIV

THOSE who have not seen those days of struggle in Russia will find it difficult to understand what had really happened, what was really happening. Consider a peasant people, a hundred millions, a peasant population that has for years been ruled by a power they never understood, but to which they submitted, a peasant population that somehow hoped that its condition would in time be ameliorated by some miraculous deed either of God or his representative on earth, the Czar. Consider a dumb peasant population that did not question or ask by what means the situation was to be changed, but hoped in their dumb way that their master or their masters would somehow, some day, if not for them for generations to come, ameliorate the conditions of the population out of the goodness of their hearts.

And suddenly came the great war. There had been many wars in which Russia had been engaged. But those were wars of which the people understood more or less the purpose and the aim. Those were wars from which

THE VOLGA BOATMAN 155

soldiers had returned and told glorious tales of victory, of the sacking of cities after sweeping everything before them, while the cannons boomed and the music played and the Cossacks with their picks and lances rode irresistibly forward.

But this was a new kind of war, a war for which no one had great enthusiasm, of which no one knew the aim or purpose, or what benefit it would bring to Russia.

And it was principally, the peasants were told, a war with Germany, with Niemtzia. And the Germans, our peasants knew, were infinitely superior to them. It was from Germany that they received their agricultural machinery. In their minds the steam locomotive and electricity, and everything which they did not understand, had originated in Germany. The doctors and the pharmacists who healed their sick were either Germans or Russians who had gone to Germany and learned these things. The superior officers of the Russian army were educated in Germany. The kniazes and their Czars, and everything that was knowledge, intelligence, was from Germany. So they knew that Germany was a formidable power with which they had been at peace till then.

And now the Czar was at war with that formidable power. The Czarina, who was herself a German woman, was against the war. The house of the Czar was divided against itself.

Every time fresh regiments of soldiers were sent to the front the Czar prayed for their success while the Czarina prayed for their defeat. And the thousands and thousands, first the very young ones and then the older ones, that were sent to the Mazurian Lakes, never came back. They were swallowed by the marshes, dying up to their necks in the mud from which they could not extricate themselves, like flies on fly paper.

And the cripples who straggled back, haggard, broken, exhausted, hollow-eyed, were speechless. There were no tales of great victory by soldiers who came back. They all said that they never set eyes on the enemy. The enemy was at a considerable distance, from where he sent annihilating iron that struck them wherever they were, that buried them without giving them any chance to fight him. It was as if a million invisible iron bands closed upon them, broke their bodies, and opened again to let their bodies fall from between the fingers.

And then after years of such destruction these peasants were told that the Czar was no more. A new government had come into being; a government without a Czar. A man like other men they had met in the towns whenever they had gone out of their villages, a lawyer, a simple man, had taken the reins of power in his hands. And the duma, the zemstvos and the soviets, had decided that soon there should be no more war with the Niemtzis. For this, the end of the war, the Russians were told, had been the cause of the change of the government. They were to be relieved of military service and sent home, those who were still alive; back to their wives and their children, back to their fields.

And there appeared amongst them in villages and hamlets and at the inns people who dared to speak and to explain to them matters. It was no longer to be "go where you are sent." The people were to be informed about this and that and the other thing. It was to be a government of the people; with representatives of the people in the Duma. It was the Lvoff government. The Lvoff government was followed by the Kerensky rule.

The French, who had proven to be as clever as the Germans, were to be their good friends along with the English. Stragglers from all parts of Russia began to return home. The roads were filled with them. They dragged themselves, cripple leaning upon cripple, the blind ones feeling their way and begging their way on the road as they continued leaning on their sticks, always going, going, going back home.

And after this state of affairs had lasted a short few months something else happened in starved and starving Russia. A new change of government. A new government that claimed to be even more liberal than the first. A government not of lawyers and city people, a government not of the mestchanin, but a government of workers, of the peasants themselves. A government in which every one of them could be a part if he only wanted. Each village was to have its own government representative. All the land belonged to them and was to be distributed equally. There were to be no more poor and no more rich. There were to be no thousand rules and laws by which a man could be sent to jail or deported to Siberia to work in the mines of Sakhalin. There were to be no more armies, no more kniazes and boyars who preyed upon them. No more usurers and business people. There

A Cecil B. De Mille Production. *The Volga Boatman.*
TERROR REIGNS WHEN THE HELPLESS ARISTOCRATS FIND THEMSELVES AT THE MERCY OF THE POWER-MADDENED REDS.

was to be no money. There was to be no poverty and no riches. Every one in Russia was to be equally as happy as the next one. And it was up to each zemstvo and each local government to arrange these things as best suited them. Factories and fields had passed into the hands of those who produced, and there was to be a definite peace with Niemtzia.

The Brest-Litovsk peace, of which many of the intelligent Russians had spoken with horror, of which many had spoken as the greatest defeat of Russia, was in the eyes of the peasants really the greatest victory. The bolsheviki won Russia by that stroke. They had the pulse of the people. What mattered it that they engaged themselves to pay to the Germans considerable sums of money. As long as they got peace and freedom out of the war before the others they were victors. Let the Germans take the rest if they so wanted.

And now not only the stragglers returned to their homes, not only the crippled and the blind, but all the soldiers crowded the roads in large gangs. They returned singing as if they had been really victorious in battle. They had gained in the battle more than a victory over the enemy. They had gained a victory over the enemy in their own country. They had gained their freedom. They had gained the right to live and be happy. People had been busy talking to them, explaining the new conditions.

They were going to have more schools and fewer churches, more schools and fewer barracks, more schools and fewer jails. They were going to instruct themselves until they should be like the Niemtzis, and have even the Niemtzis tremble before them.

And those who argued against these ideas paid with their lives. The men for whom the dream of brotherly love had suddenly been realized knew neither pity nor quarter. What happened to the palace of Kniaz Nikita happened to a thousand other palaces. What happened to Kniaz Nikita himself happened to hundreds of others. Those who were not quick enough to realize what was pending for them, those who were not quick enough to perceive and run away while there was yet time paid for their temerity with their lives. Russia was a charnal house, a mad house run by millions of mad men. Those of the nobility who fled with whatever they could lay their hands on are now spread all over the world. Barons and counts, princes and noblemen of all kinds, acting as valets and chauffeurs, working in factories and in stores all over the world, but not in Russia.

And it was of this revolution, of this mad house making, that Ivan was a part. He had from the very beginning, it is true, doubted whether the Russians were fit to accept this happiness; whether the Russians knew how to take advantage of it, whether coming suddenly as it had come it would not destroy them before making them happy.

When you are thirsty you need water enough to drink. But when much water comes you must know how to swim. It is not all to be drunk up. And Ivan had been afraid that the Russians would attempt to drink all the water and drown themselves within. At times he felt as if the newly found freedom was destroying the whole population. And yet at other times another spirit would seize him and he would think differently. The orgy of the newly found freedom would play itself out. The Russians would find themselves and return to work, and work out their salvation on the fields and in shops with the newly obtained freedom.

One had to choose one's orientation in Russia. One was either for or against the revolution. One was either on the side of the people or on the side of the enemy who wanted to bring back the old order of things. There was no middle way. Kerensky was not wrong. Only he should have waited until after the bolsheviki had ruled Russia for six months instead of coming before them.

But even in Ivan's greatest enthusiasm doubts would assail him. He could not think, as many others thought, that the kniazes and the military people and the people of the czar and all the aristocrats were monsters, all of them. He did not believe that there was not anything good in them, and that they were to be treated like monsters. And it was this spirit of doubt, quite as much as the loveliness and the youth and the courage of Vera, while he was standing before her ready to shoot her, which made him save her.

And during the days he spent with her, traveling in the gypsy cart, he learned to appreciate her even more than during the few fateful moments. She spoke to him on the way, and from what she said he knew that her heart bled for Russia. Sheltered as she had been in her home, blurred as her perceptions had been by all the things she had learned and by the life she had lived in her palace, she did not think that things could be very different.

All the happiness of the people was to come from above, and as much as she could give them she had given. The happiness of the Russian peasant depended on the heart of his master. That was her idea. She hoped that they all had good masters. What Russia needed was culture for the masters. That was her idea.

Ivan knew that she was as good a Russian as he was, that the people who had always been starving in misery were not better Russians than the ones who had always fed on the best of the land. That all happiness was a way of thinking, not riches, not poverty.

And when she left Ivan to go to her own people his despair of losing her was even deeper than he could show. It was not only the despair of losing a woman for whom he has conceived a passion of love. How different his feeling for her from the lust he had conceived for Mariusha. It was not that at all, it was the feeling that he had of becoming her enemy that hurt so terribly. Belonging as they did to two separate classes, to two contending forces, they were mortal enemies.

And then came the first great defeat of the Denikin army. The enemies of the revolution were routed and thousands of them were captured. And though Ivan was no traitor to his own class he began to think continually of Vera. He feared that she had also been caught in the net spread for the anti-revolutionists, and wished frequently that it had not happened, that her party had not been defeated. He could not sleep of nights imagining her somewhere in a dungeon, somewhere where they were torturing her in order to make her give up the secrets of their organization. There were days when in the midst of all things he would suddenly imagine seeing her before him, haggard, worn, tortured, facing a squad of soldiers ready to shoot her down.

Yet Ivan had taken up Feodor's work. He was going around and talking everywhere, explaining to the peasants the new régime. No one knew better than Ivan that though the bolsheviki had seemingly won over the country, many peasants were as hostile to them, now that they had their land, as peasants have always been hostile to city folk. They welcomed the advantage that was put into their hands after the land had been given them, but they did not intend to, and would not, share what they had with city people. Talk as they would Russia was torn inwardly by the cleav-

THE VOLGA BOATMAN

age between the city and the rural population. They were hostile to one another. The bolsheviki had given to the peasants the land, the food of the country, and the peasants realized they had the upper hand.

And there were peasants around the rich regions who had much more than they could consume. While the people in the cities were starving the peasants kept on complaining that they too should get their share of what was coming from other countries to relieve the starvation in Russia. Many of them had hidden stores of food, that they trafficked with.

And it was his mission not to take it away from them by force but to make them understand that from then on they and the city people were one body. That they were no longer to look upon the others as enemies if they did not want the city people to look upon them as enemies. And Ivan succeeded in many instances in convincing them. For you can do many things with a Russian if you only talk to him appealingly. In Russia the man with a pleasing voice wins. It does not matter what you say as long as they like your voice.

In a short time the revolutionary leaders saw his utility. He was taken into their councils. He became a sort of representative of them to the zemstvos of the villages; an ambulant representative, going from one place to the other as he pleased. And he did all this with great zeal because he wanted to win the confidence of the leaders, so that he should be able to go into jails and dungeons and look for Vera, and be of assistance to her.

And it was while he was thus employed that he learned all about the great power of Stephan. And the power of Mariusha who had married him. He also heard all details about the terrible traitor they were looking for high and low. Not only Stephan and Mariusha searched for Ivan, but a good many of the tcheka forces inquired everywhere, snooped and spied to get hold of the terrible man that had betrayed them once and was probably betraying them again.

There were no end of tales about what he had done. The incident of his saving Vera was exaggerated in order to excuse a great many things. The tale went that Ivan had come down with a whole army to save her, and that he had killed a number of men in doing so. No wonder that they were looking everywhere for him. He was the great traitor of the revolution.

THE VOLGA BOATMAN 167

And it was from the tcheka people that he heard all about Dmitri Ivanof and his cruelty, and his prowess. For by that time Dmitri Ivanof had gained the leadership of the anti-revolutionary forces.

And there were tales about the woman he was in love with. And they knew she was the daughter of Kniaz Nikita. And then, tortured by jealousy and hate, Ivan could not help thinking about her. He could not help hoping that when she should be in straits as she was certain to be because the bolsheviki were continually advancing victoriously in spite of the foreign help the anti-revolutionists received from several sources, he could not help feeling that if anything should happen he would be only too willing to be of assistance to her, too willing to save her at the risk of his own life. He was ready to go before any council and tell them that while she might be on the other side, erringly, it was so because she held a mistaken opinion. Yet he knew she was as good a Russian as anybody. He was ready to give himself completely away and tell the story of how and why he had saved her. He would have been only too willing to stand before any revolutionary tribunal and tell them how a real Russian woman felt even a minute before her death.

But nothing of the sort happened. He became more and more influential in the councils of the revolutionary leaders as his usefulness as an ambulant propagandist grew, and as his reputation in that direction increased. By the time the Odessa incident happened he had strong friends everywhere. Brought before the tribunal of any revolutionary force, he could have explained everything and gotten a fair meed of justice. As much justice as Russia could mete out in those days, torn as she was by inner struggles, wary as she was of betrayals, which were only too common. In those days a suspected man was much better a dead man. He was frequently put away because it was the better part. If he was suspected it was better to kill him instead of letting him free and having two, three, four or any number of people trailing him.

Ivan was of course unwilling to be caught by the tcheka in Odessa because he knew that he would fall into Stephan's hands. He could not expect justice or understanding there. From the tales he had heard about Mariusha, and knowing her as he did, and remembering what she had told him would happen if he ever left her, or betrayed her, he knew how swift the judgment against him would be. Frequently Stephan first killed the accused and then pronounced judgment against him. It was much easier, much more expedient that way, he argued.

Even amongst the bolshevik leaders it was whispered that once the necessary period of terror was over, men like Stephan and others of his kind would have to be put away somewhere. That he and his kind were like a certain poison, which after being used for healing purposes had to be safely put away, lest the ones using it should poison themselves with it.

A whole lot of Stephans had grown up like mushrooms all over the country. All the cruelty of the muzhiks seemed to have distilled itself into these men. All that was base and beastly centered itself into the hearts of the men of the tcheka.

Beasts like that were not only on the Bolshevik side. The anti-revolutionary forces had just as many.

All the Stephans of the Russian people were equally divided between both forces. There were Stephans and Dmitri Ivanofs from one end of Russia to the other. All of them would be put away like lepers on an island after the revolution should be over; that they kill and destroy one another or that they perish in isolation there.

And not only men, but there were women aplenty as cruel as Stephan and Dmitri Ivanof. There was one woman at Nijni Novgorod who had made for herself a reputation as a killer. You would have sworn that she was the mildest creature if you had looked at her. While the bolsheviki were a secret party and she belonged to it many had thought her a saint. She had innocent blue eyes and a high forehead, and the sweetest mouth ever. That woman would wield a revolver as if it were a fan. She pulled that trigger with an ecstasy on her face as if she were singing a song that she had just composed. She killed in ecstatic moments only. She was tribunal, judge and executioner.

And in the Kolchak army there were many of that type too. Most of these people had not realized that while they apparently fought for a principle they had always been fighting for the privilege of killing, for the privilege of exercising their inborn cruel natures.

CHAPTER XV

After Ivan had escaped from that coffee house in Odessa, while the two contending forces were slashing at one another, he knew that something more serious had happened than was apparent. His identity had been disclosed. And the worst of that was not the fact that he should have to lie low and hide from the tens of thousands of people who knew him by sight, and from the number of friends that he had made during his activity, the worst of it was that he could no longer hope to be of any help in case Vera should be in straits. For the tcheka would surely be advised everywhere about his existence and betrayal. And he knew that it would take an even longer time to explain if he were called on to explain than it would have taken before. And Russians had no time for explanations. Russia said: "I doubt you, Brother. Therefore I kill you."

Twice within ten days Odessa and that region passed from the hands of one force into the hands of the others. And both times Odessa was treated as an enemy city by those who captured it, with the slaughter going on for hours, each one trying to impose his rule by a reign of terror headed by Stephans and Dmitri Ivanofs.

Ivan lay low, hidden and disguised, during the invasions and retreats. His heart shrank with every victory, with every defeat. And still, hunted animal as he was, he hoped that he might catch a glimpse of Vera, and still he hoped that he might be of assistance to her.

The last time the White forces seemed to have entrenched themselves solidly. Indeed they felt themselves so strongly in possession of the city that they relented a little and even issued an ukase in which they declared they were willing to forgive the population of the city its former friendliness to the bolsheviki, its former submission to the bolsheviki, if the population of the city was ready to be with them and to consider them the masters.

It seemed as if they were going to start out from there, spreading all over Russia, but a well-organized Red force came swooping down upon them.

In the street fighting that followed between the contending forces Ivan hastily dressed in the uniform of a fallen Red soldier and joined their forces. He knew that these soldiers had been hastily banded together, that there were no regiments and battalions which, organized under individual officers, would recognize their soldiers. And so together with the Red forces he fought for the recapture of the city. They won.

Stephan and Mariusha appeared not long after that in Odessa and set up their tribunal. And if an anti-revolutionist had terrorized Odessa into submission before that, it was Stephan's turn now to do better than he did. On the one hand his cruelties and on the other hand Mariusha with a band of gypsies, well-fed and well-dressed, behaving as if they were in the high councils of the bolsheviki themselves, were fattening themselves by robbing right and left, with Mariusha being of tremendous assistance to them.

The gypsies would go to a merchant they knew and mulct him of all the gold and jewels in his possession under the threat of bringing him before the dreaded tribunal. And when it was thought that the victim had not given up all that he possessed he was arrested, and then all his relatives would come to his rescue, and each one poured his jewels and his wealth out into the laps of the gypsies to buy the freedom of the man.

Stephan was innocent of this. He was too much absorbed in his own passion to know that the woman beside him was trafficking with his cruelty and his power, to know that the people of the women for whom alone he had love and passion were doing what they did. Stephan was an honest monster. His passion for bolshevik justice amounted to a religious fanaticism.

The gypsies knew everybody in town, and especially the rich Jewish merchants. They had played before at the weddings of these people and had appraised their wealth.

There were merchants whose sons and daughters were high in the councils of the bolsheviki, busy propagating and strengthening the rule of the party they had always been in favor of. And the fathers and mothers of these sons and daughters were robbed and tortured until they disclosed all the wealth they had hidden. Officially there was no distinction in Russia between Jew and Gentile. A good many of the Jews were at the head of the government in power. But unofficially they were now despoiled more than ever. The

Jews at the head of the government had to show that they made no distinction.

They were the merchants of the city, and had the gold and the jewels which a good many of other Stephans coveted.

And when the anti-revolutionary forces had come into Odessa they fell upon the Jews and robbed them and tortured them; it was their theory that the Jews were at the bottom of all the trouble in Russia; that the Jews were the ones who had brought bolshevism and had tumbled them down from the high power in which they had sat enthroned for centuries.

Nothing was more pitiful than to see these old people between the upper and nether millstone, ground down and tortured for no reason at all except that they were what they were. Here is the story of the Abram family, who owned a large shoe leather shop. The Abrams had one son and one daughter, both of whom had been released from the dungeon in which they had been thrown by the Czar years before for their revolutionary activities, when the revolutionary force came into power. They were both high in the councils of Moscow. They were extremists, idealists who believed in the distribution of all the wealth to all the people.

And then the Whites came into town. And as the Abrams were denounced as being the father and mother of the dreaded revolutionists, the old people were immediately taken to jail by the anti-revolutionist forces. Tortured, harassed, and questioned day and night. The mother died in the jail within a few days. And before the same thing had happened to the father the Whites had to run away and leave the city in the hands of the Reds. The daughter of the Abrams returned to Odessa just in time to bury her mother. Her mother was a martyr to her ideal. And the hatred against the Whites in her breast must have grown a thousand times stronger than it had ever been. Then she left for Moscow. Duty called her.

In the taking and the retaking of the city, when Stephan came again into power, old Abram was denounced as a spy by Mariusha's people. He was a capitalist. He had hidden his wealth. He trafficked. They accused him of all the things without ever giving the old man a chance to explain himself. Finally he, too, died in jail. And his son, who had been sent for by the relatives, arrived just in time to see the burial of the father.

Tragedies of the kind were very frequent

in those days in Russia, but the one that centered around the Abram family seems to epitomize what happened everywhere.

* * * * *

Russia is a land of miracles. What happens in Russia can happen nowhere else. What cannot happen in any other country happens in Russia. During the war the Russians had captured whole regiments of the Austrian army, chiefly composed of Czechs. Now these Czechs, though they were Austrian subjects, were anything but friendly to the Austrians, and were greatly in sympathy with the Allies, although they fought under the Austrian flag. They surrendered themselves to the Russians to avoid fighting under the enemy's flag against their friends.

When the revolution came the attention of the new government was drawn to the tens of thousands of Czechs quartered anywhere from the middle of Russia up to Siberia. When the bolsheviki came into power they treated their nominal prisoners with great kindness. They allowed these Czechs to walk around the town free and unfettered as if they were Russians. The only thing the bolsheviki did not allow them was to carry arms.

These Czechs were anxious to fight again,

and hoped to be able to fight again on the side of the Allies against their erstwhile masters. This the bolsheviki opposed. It was decided that they should not be allowed to carry arms. Russia had had enough of war and was not anxious to augment the Allied forces with the thousands of Czechs.

But meanwhile the White forces under Denikin, supported as they were by the Allies, as well as the Kolchak forces in Siberia, had armed the Czechs. And then there was the great phenomenon of prisoners of war actually taking possession of part of the country in which they had been imprisoned, and ruling it. Needless to say, the anti-revolutionary forces, the officers' party, all who were against the bolshevik rule, helped the Czechs secretly and overtly when they took possession of a town.

What actually happened in Jaroslav when the Czechs came in was unforgettable. The Red army was not yet well organized. It was just a rabble of people, badly led, badly disciplined, who did not know where their heads were, badly armed, badly nourished, and who had not yet learned what friendly authority means.

They were a loud-mouthed rabble, singing

revolutionary songs. When the Czechs, ten thousand strong, entered Jaroslav, uniformed, disciplined, the Reds put up only a semblance of an opposition before they fled and left the town in the hands of the erstwhile prisoners.

The populace of Jaroslav, composed as it was mostly of merchants, met the Czechs who had taken possession of the city with bands of music and threw flowers at them from the windows and the doors. For a few days the Czechs, who had a good deal of information of what was going on in Jaroslav before, and who were given more information by that part of the populace that was friendly to them, set out on an orgy of cruelties and punishments. All the former commissars of the city were speared and shot mercilessly without even the semblance of judgment. All those who had been reported favorable to the bolsheviki were thrown into dungeons and jails where they were left to die of hunger and disease.

When they thought they had established their rule solidly the Czechs, who had now been augmented by a great number of officers of the Whites, began to give their balls. And Ivan, who had thought that Jaroslav had been pretty well denuded of jewelry and wealth that had seemingly swelled the coffers of the bolsheviki, saw with his own eyes how little truth there had been in the report. At the first ball a great deal of sparkling jewelry came to the fore.

Ivan had hidden and disguised himself with some newly found friends among the American Y. M. C. A., who happened to be there, and who remained during the bolshevik régime and continued while the Czechs were there with the same equanimity, distributing bread and flour to the poor regardless of their political opinions and beliefs. His host, who later on played an important rôle as intermediary between the bolsheviki and the American government, a charming man, took Ivan with him as his driver to one of these balls. There was a gypsy band playing. Ivan remained outside at first, listening to the hilarious laughter of the women caused by the champagne that was running freely, and the loud outbursts of the officers.

But when he heard the strains of music it seemed to him that he had heard these strains before. There was something in the quality of the music that he recognized. He looked through the window into the well-lit room, for if he remained in Jaroslav after the bolshevik forces had been driven out, it was chiefly because he hoped against all probabilities that he might again catch a glimpse of Vera.

She was not there, but he recognized the gypsies. There were two of Mariusha's tribe in the band. He watched them closely for over half an hour, and he noted how they had their eyes fixed on the jewels the people wore. They took note of everything so as to know later on.

There was another ball the following day, and the bolsheviki were reported routed. The Czechs assured the population they would march to Moscow together with Denikin's army and take possession of the government, to return it to the old flag, to bring back Russia into the fold of the Allies to fight against the Germans. More jewelry, more wine, more wealth, more luxury, was brought to the fore at the next ball. And while it lasted, while the Czechs were at Jaroslav, there was ball after ball, and more and more of the wealth that had been hidden at the approach of the bolsheviki came to the fore.

The gypsies meanwhile made note of all they saw. Ivan shuddered thinking what would happen if the Czechs should suddenly be driven out of Jaroslav and the Reds should come in; if Stephan were again to be established as the head of the revolutionary tribunal.

How the blood would flow! The dungeons would fill with men and women. Ivan had no doubt that the gypsies who had remained there would willingly, anxiously, act as informers. And who could know better than they did who possessed costly jewels, who was friendly with the White army, who was friendly with the anti-revolutionary forces? They were in possession of the most valuable information. Denunciation meant fortunes for them. Mariusha would help.

He debated with himself whether he should not tell these things to his friend the American. Perhaps, he thought, it would be better to get the gypsies out of town and save as far as was possible the lives of people in the event of the return of the bolsheviki.

Yet after all, Ivan belonged to the Reds. He belonged to the party of the people. Would Feodor have done that? He hated himself. Would Feodor have acted that way? It would have been treason. He had already enough on his head without additional sin. Still, he shuddered and debated and doubted,

THE VOLGA BOATMAN 183

knowing that if he told what he knew to his American friend he would have immediately intervened. And he knew what would have happened to the gypsies. The Czechs and their friends had plenty of bullets, and they would be anxious to make a clean job of it. The gypsies as well as a good many others would have augmented the heap of dead bodies that was daily thrown into quicklime graves.

Meanwhile the reports about the success of the White army in combination with that of the Czechs were given hourly. They were going triumphantly forward. The Red army fled before them. Nothing was to stop the White forces from getting to Moscow, nothing was to stop them from getting possession of the whole of Russia.

The rule of the bolsheviki was at an end. Those were the reports. But what was really happening was that the Czechs and the Whites forgot themselves in the few towns which they had occupied. The officers drank and feasted and amused themselves with the women at balls and parties given in their honor. While this was going on in their camp Trotzky had taken a hand in the organizing of the Red army. Again what could never have happened in any other country happened in Russia. It is a country of miracles. An inexperienced man undertook to organize an army in a country where the army had been defeated. He undertook to officer that army with officers who were originally the enemies of the party of which this man was at the head, but who were good enough Russians to realize that it was far better that Russia should govern itself, no matter what party governed it, than that strangers should govern it even if those strangers happened to be of the same opinion that they themselves were.

Systematically and quietly all the munition factories were opened and put in running order again. Quietly but firmly an army was being organized and disciplined, even while the enemy was feasting and rejoicing in his victories. Those youngsters who were now drawn into the army, fed, clothed and treated much better than they had ever expected to be treated, were pliant and obeyed the orders of the superiors, though they addressed them as Tavarish. It was friendly authority with the accent on the authority. And these peasants who had been trained to obey for generations and generations found in obedience relief of doubt, relief of responsibility.

There were a thousand rumors afloat everywhere of the successes of the White army. It seemed impossible to those even who were in favor of the bolshevik government that anything would stop the onward march of the White army. And rumors were afloat daily of how the bolsheviki had flown and run away, of how thousands had been captured.

Trotzky was biding his time. He knew the psychology of the Russian people. He knew that the more miraculous his first coup would be, the greater the effect. It was not a question of merely opposing an enemy or of having him retreat a few hundred yards. It was a different kind of an enemy. An enemy of the spirit. It was far better to wait until one could strike a decisive blow when nobody should expect it, a blow that would have the force to crush the enemy at once in its impact, a blow that would impress the whole of Russia and have the effect of augmenting the Red army with volunteers who would come of themselves to join it. Trotzky sensed how eager the whole Russian youth was to join and be in a victorious army; they who had been so cruelly defeated in the last few years.

You can change a country's political attitude. You can change a country's economic condition. But you cannot eradicate at once in the young men the militaristic instinct; the desire for feats of arms, the desire for conquest and victory. And Trotzky knew this, and he waited. He comes from a patient people, a people that has outlived all its conquerors.

When the time came the blow of the Red army was struck. Everything crumpled up before them like an edifice of straw under a sledge hammer. Ivan had heard rumors of a Red army being organized, and right on top of these rumors came the news of the first blow they had struck. He could see the sudden change in the anxiety of the people of Jaroslav, and the demeanor of the White soldiers who were in town. The soldiers and the people looked uneasy, but the officers, sure as they were of another victory, continued their feasts and their balls until orders should come for them to advance. Life was too sweet and too easy for them to worry about that rabble of a Red army. There were beautiful women in Jaroslav. There was much champagne and good food. The gypsies played passionate music. Life was sweet and easy.

And then the blow was struck at Jaroslav itself. From where and how nobody shall ever know! The blow was struck during a great ball given by the officers in order to reassure the populace.

"There is no danger. See, we amuse ourselves."

While the officers were dancing with the bejeweled ladies and the music was playing, while champagne was flowing, cannon shots were heard. Almost at the same moment the ball room, which had been lit brilliantly by electricity, became dark. There were screams and cries everywhere, and loud calls of the officers for light. Matches were struck here and there, flashlights appeared. People began to rush out in their ball costumes, many of them with their clothes torn, running through the streets. There were many whose ear lobes were ripped open by hands too impatient to unscrew the earrings.

Loud trumpet calls were blown through the streets. The whole city, which had been lit brilliantly, was plunged in darkness of a sudden, while cannon were booming and the trumpets called the White soldiers and the Czech soldiers to assemble.

That night Jaroslav was entered by the Red army. And then in the morning the real carnage began. The bolsheviki entered the city. After a few days of comparative quiet, during which the city was plastered with posters announcing how the populace should behave and what was expected of it, the revolutionary tribunal began to function.

Because of the rapidity with which the coup was made many of the merchants who had unearthed their wares and put them in the stores to sell while the White forces were in Jaroslav had had no time to secrete them again. The newly arrived army refrained from plunder, they refrained from any brutality, merely patrolling the streets quietly day and night. It looked like a dead city. No one ventured outside. No one of those who had feasted the Czechs or the White army dared to show their faces anywhere. But after the revolutionary tribunal had begun to function, military patrols would stop in front of a house, two men would go into it and emerge from it with a whole family that was taken between bayonets to headquarters.

And again Ivan saw the work of the gypsies.

And again the work of the Y. M. C. A. went on quietly and impartially, distributing bread to the needy who dared to go out in the street to form a line in front of the office where the bread and flour were being distributed to them. As the driver of the Y. M. C. A., wearing American clothes, Ivan was more or less secure, as well as disguised. Yet he never felt secure enough or disguised well enough for the gypsies. Hundreds of them seemed to spring up from everywhere as though they had come together with the Red army. And not long afterwards he learned that Mariusha was in town, though Stephan was not at the head of the Jaroslav secret tribunal.

CHAPTER XVI

WITH the pliancy of youth and the pliancy of a gypsy, able to adapt herself to all conditions and all surroundings, Mariusha adapted herself to her new situation in life. And in so adapting herself she also compelled Stephan to adapt himself better than he otherwise would have done. From a gypsy girl who had roamed through the country she became a more or less intelligent woman, the wife of a man in high authority. She dressed considerably quieter than she had dressed before. She mingled freely with the wives of the people in high authority among the bolsheviki, and by her charm and her beautiful voice she gained their confidence and admiration. As most of these women were of the intellectual type she acquired from them a smattering sufficient to cover up her real ignorance of the things she was continually talking about. There was no need for her to hide her birth. There had come a revulsion of feeling toward gypsies. Instead of being humbled and considered as half savages, from whom one had

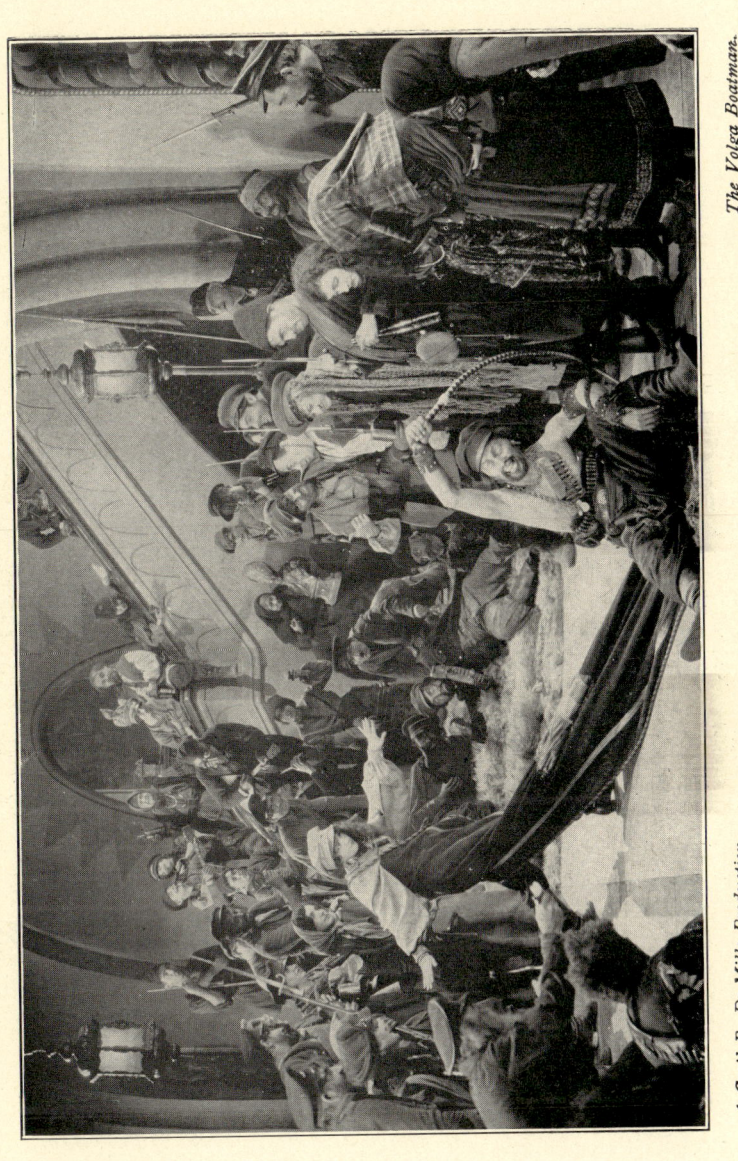

A Cecil B. De Mille Production.   *The Volga Boatman.*
THE REVOLUTIONISTS REVEL IN THE CASTLE, WHILE MARIUSHA AND STEPHAN ENTERTAIN THEM WITH A WILD, SPONTANEOUS DANCE.

everything to fear, these people who now governed Russia began to look upon gypsies as a colorful people, and began to pay much more attention to their romantic qualities than they had paid before.

Mariusha was in their eyes an even finer creature because of her gypsy origin. It seemed to them that they had newly discovered in Mariusha's people a people who had suffered even more than the peasants during the régime of the Czar and the aristocracy. It was only fitting justice, poetic justice, that a daughter of such people should take part in the political life of the reorganized country.

And she was a wonderfully civilized being, they all asserted, a civilized being with temperament and charm. A civilized being who could talk eloquently and had a beautiful voice. What more does a Russian want? You can talk a Russian into anything. Of course it was considered a pity that she was the wife of Stephan, who, although by everybody considered of great use, was never regarded otherwise than as a hangman; a hangman necessary for the enforcement of the bolshevik rule, but a hangman nevertheless, who should be retired when his office should no longer be necessary.

Underneath the veneer of civilization, underneath the veneer of revolution, underneath all this one single thought animated Mariusha. She wanted revenge. She was still the gypsy that she had been born. It was all make believe now, as it had ever been with her. It was the gypsy ability to act. Gypsies can apparently be humble and submissive, like slaves, until you would think you do them a favor by stepping upon them, that they longed for nothing else but to be stepped upon. Yet underneath this their spirit would boil while their lips smile and their voices are humble and flattering. When opportunity comes the vengeance is more cruel than the humiliation had been. Playing with gypsies is not playing with fire, it is playing with lightning, poison water, fire and storms combined.

And the need was of making herself into a being different from what she was before. So she did it. She had learned well the part she was acting. She was talking about the poor, starving peasants that the bolsheviki were going to help. She was speaking with hatred about the wealthy aristocrats who had so misruled Russia for so many years. It was playing, whatever she said and whatever she did. Underneath it all she was thinking of only one thing, that was to fulfill her gypsy vow to kill Ivan if he ever left her. That was the uppermost thought in her mind. That was the only thing towards which she strove.

Stephan, power, the acquisition of friends, jewels, Russia, White Russia, Red Russia, aristocrats, bolsheviki, mattered nothing to her. All these things were temporary things of very little importance. Gypsies have lived through many changes in this world. They have seen kings come and go, governments come and go. They place no value on things outside their own life.

What was important was her vow, next to her fidelity to her own tribe and her own conscience. And as day passed after day without her being able to fulfill her vow, her hatred grew even stronger than it had been. No matter what might happen to her, no matter to what position she would have raised herself, she could even have become the Czar of Russia, still it would not have satisfied her, still it would have been only a temporary thing, until her own hand should sink the dagger into Ivan's breast. All these things would be temporary, inconsequential, until she had avenged herself.

* * * * *

Meanwhile Vera was leading a most harassing life of doubt and fear. Dmitri Ivanof, whose power among his people grew from day to day, saw his reputation increase with his cruelties. Once his passions aroused and the baser nature come to the surface, with all the polish of civilization and culture gone, he showed himself to be the brute that he really was. He who fought and he who led those who seemingly were fighting for the maintenance of the old order of things, telling the world that they wanted to save Russia for civilization, that they wanted to save Russia from the primitiveness of the bolsheviki, who were to return Russia to hundreds of years back, the nobleman was really the one who retrograded hundreds of years back in his attempt to keep a woman, who did not love him, by fear and brute force.

And when they had taken possession of the town of Nijm he installed her in the house of a very rich man who had been executed because he was accused of having sympathized with the bolsheviki. At any rate his children were bolsheviki. It was in that house that Vera heard discussions about the triumphs and the defeats in the field, of the ambitions and the plans that were laid down to squelch the bolsheviki and to wrest the power from them. And Vera doubted. The same doubts that assailed Ivan when he saw the bolsheviki in power, the same doubts that assailed him when he saw the pettiness of the little commissars, henchmen and hangmen, all these petty little czars that had grown up under the bolshevik government, the same doubts assailed Vera now about the ruling fitness of the people she saw about her.

Perhaps Ivan epitomized for her the class of people the White forces were fighting, as she epitomized for him the other side which his people were fighting. There were times when she was much more convinced of the Russianism of the bolsheviki than of the people of her own class. For of her own people, she knew that they had associated with the Czechs, with foreigners, practically the enemies of Russia, in order to succeed. She knew that they were bartering with all the nationalities, giving them concessions of timber and oil for ammunition with which to destroy and kill their own people.

And her doubts were not relieved when she knew more. Back of the White army were Russian officers, Czech officers, French officers. In the army of Kolchak things were not different from the army of Denikin. Russians were strangling one another, each one in the name of a better Russia, of a greater Russia than he had been born in.

She was many a time tempted to unburden her soul to Dmitri Ivanof. She thought after all that it could not be that all his best sentiments had simply disappeared as in quicksand. She had loved the man. She had not yet torn him out of her heart. She still loved him, though she hated him for what he was doing. She thought that underneath his cruelty there was a different man. It was her great mistake that she had taken for depth that which was really only on the surface. Instead of thinking that everything he had shown of himself before was only a veneer which had been rubbed off at the first impact with life, she thought that the way he behaved now was only a veneer, while the real man lay down deep under the surface, a fine, gentle soul that had to be recalled to come to life.

She made several attempts to talk to him when he came to visit her. She asked him to sit down near her and quite unconsciously assumed the same manner and voice which she had had before the great calamity came upon Russia.

"Sit down near me, Dmitri Ivanof, like this. Now let's talk French as we used to talk. There are so many things I want to tell you."

And Dmitri Ivanof would seemingly return to be the Dmitri Ivanof who had been before. Only in one respect, however.

"Have you finally decided that you love me, Vera?" he asked, with tender voice. "Vera! Vera!" And his eyes would become moist.

"No, it is not about that that I was going to talk to you, Dmitri Ivanof. It is about Russia."

"Oh, about Russia," he exclaimed, half disgusted. And instantly his voice would grow cold and he would talk Russian.

"About Russia I shall talk only in Russian," was his answer.

"But Dmitri Ivanof—"

"No, Vera. It is not about such things that I want to talk to women and listen to women talk to me. I have come to ask you again, when are we getting married?"

"I shall never marry you as long as this carnage goes on," Vera answered.

"Shall you marry me when we enter Moscow?" he asked her.

"Enter Moscow!" She shrugged her shoulders. "And how about staying there. How long do you think you can stay there? And will it be a Czechs' Moscow, or a French Moscow? Whose Moscow do you think it will be?"

These were the conversations that took place every time the two of them were together. Practically the same words were spoken because the same thoughts animated these conversations. She wanted to talk about Russia and he wanted to talk about marriage.

There were times in which people came running to her, begging her to intervene; old bearded Jews, reputable merchants of the town. Their wives, crying bitterly, asked her intercession. Why should they be persecuted? Why should they be tortured? What had they done? Why had Dmitri Ivanof thrown them in dungeons? Because a son or a daughter, or some other relative, was a bolshevik or reputed to be a bolshevik? And Vera would cry together with them. Yes, why?

And then she would go to Dmitri Ivanof and intercede in those people's behalf, trying to beg him to listen carefully to all that was said. But he would answer:

"You see, these people take it for granted that you are to be my wife. They already ask you to intercede with me. 'And if I should decide to be lenient with Abramson, for instance, what then?"

And she could not. It was as if she would soil herself. As if she would barter herself away for somebody else. It was this barter that he continually offered that revolted her. And she would go home and wait and cry, knowing that because she had refused to give herself to Dmitri the victim he had in his power was suffering, was being tortured. And the men's wives were sent for by Dmitri Ivanof's henchmen and told:

"Go to Vera and ask her to come and beg Dmitri Ivanof. Let her beg Dmitri Ivanof and everything will be all right."

And they would go again and throw themselves at her feet, and beg and cry and weep. They could not understand why the Barishna, who was so good, who cried and wept together with them, who knelt near them as they attempted to kneel at her feet, they could not understand why the Barishna should refuse to help them.

After Dmitri Ivanof had discovered how much such things upset her he used them deliberately over and over again. He would throw women in dungeons and ask their husbands to go to intercede for them with Vera. He would throw young girls in dungeons and young boys, in the continual reign of terror and torture. And still Vera refused to marry him or otherwise let him possess her.

In the midst of this terror the news about Stephan and the bolshevik régime was retold and exaggerated. They wondered and cried out in astonishment and horror about the deeds of the tcheka and spread them all over the country, indeed all over the world, as examples of great brutality. But they kept quiet about their own crimes.

And so Vera, after having withstood such strain for months and months, realized it would be impossible for her to exist under the situation much longer. She realized that he had worn her down to the point where she would either have to commit murder or suicide or give herself away to the lust of Dmitri Ivanof. Then she decided to make her way out of the White lines into the Red, regardless of what was to befall her.

And then again the thought came to her about that man who had saved her. To her Ivan represented the bolsheviki, just as to him she represented the White side.

CHAPTER XVII

SPURRED by Mariusha, the gypsies had begun to look for Ivan in the cities occupied by the Whites. They had become convinced that he was to be found there. And there were also many other reasons why some of them, a large tribe, preferred to stay among the Whites than remaining among the bolsheviki. After having plundered on the other side, they began to find it more and more difficult to get out of the country to sell the jewels and the silks that they had robbed and stolen everywhere. In the cities governed by the anti-revolutionary forces there was a market for all the stolen things; an illicit market, on the outside of coffee houses and stores, where things were bartered away for a tenth of their real worth. There they could get gold coin for the jewels they possessed, which were of no use to them as long as they were in bolshevik Russia.

After a time a group of them discovered the existence of Vera. Knowing as they did all about her and how she had been saved, they figured that Ivan must be in the neighborhood and therefore they were continually spying on her. She was being watched day and night. Her movements were being noted continually by some one or other of the gypsy tribe, without it being noticed by others. Several times one of the gypsy women had introduced herself into the house under the pretext of telling her fortune. And Vera, to revive the memories of the old days, let her come to her. And the gypsy, who knew what she knew, began to allude to many things that gave Vera a starting jump. She began to wonder whether it was true that these children of the road and the desert possessed the quality of knowing the past and could foresee the future.

"You have been saved once," the old gypsy woman told her. "You have been near death once, very near death. It was a dark room. And a man was ready to kill you. And you knew that that man was ready to kill you. And then you were saved. The man saved you. I do not know how but you were saved. Tell me, isn't that so?"

Vera threw her head back. She was on the verge of a fainting spell. And the gypsy's face was so intense, as if she did not know, as if she wanted confirmation from her.

THE VOLGA BOATMAN 203

"Tell me more," Vera begged. "What more do you know? Tell me. Tell me."

"If you could tell me where the man who has saved you is I could tell you more."

Vera did not see the subterfuge and did not see that the woman was trying to obtain information from her.

"I do not know," she answered. "Perhaps you could tell me. I wish I knew. I wish I knew."

But gypsies, who are always telling fortunes by allusions, never believe what other people tell them in a direct manner. That gypsy woman did not believe Vera when she said she did not know where I was. She was certain Vera had taken an oath not to tell. So she resolved to bide her time now that she had gained the confidence of the Barishna.

There was great joy amongst the gypsies when she reported her partial success. They were soon to get the bag of diamonds from Mariusha, and perhaps more than that.

She returned again and again. There were conferences amongst the gypsies, during which that particular gypsy who had gained access to Vera was instructed what to say and what to do to the Barishna. They felt that they were near their victim. That if they were only able to keep it up they could lay their hands on the man and bring him to Mariusha and get the promised recompense; the bag of diamonds she had promised if Ivan were to be delivered to her.

It was but natural for Vera, when she had made up her mind to run away from where she was, to think of the gypsy woman, and ask her to help her get away. There were again conferences between the gypsies, though the fortune teller had asked Vera to get herself ready, that she was going to help her.

"I know where you want to go," the gypsy woman told her. "You want to go to the man who has saved your life, to that good man who has saved your life. Isn't that so, Barishna? I know. I know."

And Vera, who wanted to get away, did not deny. "Maybe."

How Vera managed to pass through the White lines is a puzzle. How the gypsies managed to leave the city without being shot at.

The day she was ready to leave the cannons had spoken again. There was a great military movement in the town. Orders were given for everybody to remain inside and not to put their heads out. When the cannon had

THE VOLGA BOATMAN

ceased to boom the tramp of horses was heard going out through the gates of the town.

The gypsy fortune teller came running to Vera and asked her to take everything she could along with her. And when several bundles had been thrown together into the waiting gypsy wagon the fortune teller still asked whether the Barishna had taken all her jewels. Then, even while the wagon was being driven through the town, the gypsy fortune teller helped Vera change her dress and put herself into one of the gypsy dresses.

There were eight or ten people all tightly packed in the wagon. First shots hit the speeding wagon from behind. And after these shots had been run away from bullets began to hit the sides of the wagon. One of the horses, harnessed troikawise, in single file, fell down. It was cut away from the harness, and the flight was continued, jerking up and down until it seemed to Vera that she was going to be thrown out through the canvas roof of the wagon.

They traveled that way till dawn. When the wagon stopped and the gypsies sprang outside Vera looked about her and did not know where she was. And it seemed to her impossible that the others knew.

Little did she realize that to these gypsies every nook and corner within hundreds of miles was as well known as the park in her own home had been known to her.

"Where are we?" she asked the one who had been telling her fortunes.

"My dear child," she said. "I'll tell you where we are. As far as you are concerned we are not far from Kazan and not far from Jaroslav and not far from Nijni Novgorod. It all depends on where you want to go."

It was only then that Vera bethought herself that she might have been trapped. It seemed to her in looking at the faces of the other gypsies that she remembered them. She did not know exactly on what occasion she had seen them before. But she knew that she had seen them before. There were a few faces in that group of the same gypsies who had played the kamarashka outside the large room in which Ivan was to kill her so that she should pay with her life for the life of Feodor.

She had been trapped. But where was she to go? Jaroslav! she decided immediately, without knowing why. Only because she had heard that Jaroslav was definitely in the hands of the bolsheviki. She expected to find Ivan there. He had saved her once. He would save her again.

And instantly the gypsies began to look with kinder eyes on her. She seemed to have given them valuable information by pronouncing the name of the city which they themselves had begun to suspect as my residence.

For three days and three nights they traveled. It seemed to Vera that they traveled in circles. And they passed several inspections of commissars. They had passes, including one that accounted for Vera's existence as a member, to show to starosties and Red patrols they encountered on the way and who asked them their destination. And when these passes were shown they were allowed to go unmolested after a few inquiries as to where the tavarish tzigans had been before and what they had observed on the way.

And the gypsies gave glib, voluble accounts of prosperous towns under the government of the bolsheviki.

Oh, everything was going to be all right. Tavarish Lenin and Tavarish Trotzky were the new czars of Russia. And they were far better czars than the former one had been.

* * * * *

On the second night the gypsy tribe had been augmented while Vera slept. Two wagons joined the first one. And the night after that another few wagons came to join theirs. How these gypsies met and why was beyond her understanding. But she knew that they looked upon her as a most valuable prize. She knew that she was virtually their prisoner. That she could not move without their observing every motion she made. And from the conversations between the gypsies and the starostes of the little villages she knew that they were on the outskirts of Jaroslav, that they had been on the outskirts of Jaroslav for some time. And she wondered why they had not gone into the town.

Occasionally one of the group would disappear and return, after hours of absence. Some sort of whispered conference would go on, and the fortune teller would come to her and ask her again whether she was certain that she could find me in Jaroslav, was this not all she desired? Vera had to find Ivan. They would help her. There was no use in going anywhere where he might not be.

And wouldn't Vera tell them how she knew that Ivan was in Jaroslav? And when Vera assured them that she did not know where

Ivan was but was going to look for him, the fortune teller shook her head and returned again to the same task a little afterwards, questioning, quizzing.

Most of the humbleness had gone out of her voice. She was subjecting Vera to as strict an interrogatory as if she was a prosecuting attorney. She would even dare to trip her up in her answers and show her contradictions. She would grow angry occasionally. At one of these sittings she even menaced Vera.

"If you won't tell me the truth," she said, "all I have to do is to tell the truth to the tavarishes we meet on the way, and then you will find out what is going to happen to you."

And then Vera knew that for some unaccountable reason these gypsies were trying to find Ivan. Vera did not know anything about his relations with Mariusha. In their flight together they had spoken but little, and then they had spoken of things that were not of their immediate lives. She could not know exactly why these gypsies should be so anxious to find him, but she knew from their behavior how anxious they were, and wondered whether it meant any good to Ivan.

"I suppose that if you were to ask one of these tavarishes that you meet on the roads,"

Vera suggested, when she was questioned closely, "they could tell us, for you say he is well known. Therefore these people might know where he is."

Finally one day they left Vera in the middle of the road in the few rags which they had given her, having taken away from her all her possessions, and departed in different directions. And though it was getting cold and the snow was falling, and the roads were deserted, Vera felt relieved to be alone, to have escaped her tormentors, to have scented danger for me.

A group of Americans passed by the road a few hours later from a journey of mercy in a village, and they picked her up. She was almost frozen when they took her in their automobile to Jaroslav.

CHAPTER XVIII

MEANWHILE Stephan had been shorn of his powers by the government of Moscow. You remember about the Abram family; how the mother had first died in jail, thrown there by the White forces because the family had been denounced as friendly to the bolsheviki, their son and daughter being high commissars of the bolshevik government. And how the father died in jail later on, when the Reds took Odessa, denounced by the gypsies as an anti-revolutionist, because they thought he had not given up all he possessed to them.

After this had happened Abram's son and daughter ran to Trotzky. And when Trotzky heard what had happened to the families of his commissars, and the danger to everybody as long as Stephan had power over life and death, the government held council. They took into consideration the fact that while the works of the tcheka and the Stephans had probably been beneficial to them in Russia, it had been largely doing them great harm outside of Russia; where the exploits of the tcheka and the cruelties of the Stephans had been denounced and written about in all the papers of the world.

The meeting between Abram's children and the other commissars must have been one at which things were threshed out thoroughly, for immediately Stephan and the other Stephans were shorn of their power and then and there it was decided to call them to account and compel them to stand trial for their cruelties. Stephan was therefore brought to Moscow and asked to wait until the commission would have time to listen to him.

* * * * *

Mariusha realized immediately that the last of Stephan's power had been used, and as he had not helped her to fulfill her vow and take her revenge, she had no further use for him, fearing also that she would have herself more than one thing to answer for when the high commission should investigate all that Stephan had done, she abandoned him and within a few days she had again lost herself in Russia with one of the tribes which were scurrying hither and thither trying to get out of the country as fast as they could before the net that was being spread should be pulled in.

Mariusha had informed them about the danger.

When most of them had left the country, Mariusha still remained within, returning from the borderline, even while her father and many of the others crossed at night over a secret path. She was so much animated by the desire to avenge herself that even her own personal danger was no consideration for her. As she could not travel alone without being detected, dressed as she was now again as a ragged gypsy, having abandoned her rather luxurious but simple clothing that she had worn while she was Stephan's wife, she induced on the promise of gold and jewels a few of her tribe to stay with her, several old women and a few men. A few days later her friends refused to stay any longer. They tried to argue, telling her that it was just as possible that I was outside of Russia as in Russia, but she would not hear of it. She was absolutely certain that Ivan was somewhere near the Volga. She knew how much the Volga attracted him, and no matter where he would be, he would still be near the river he had lived on for so many years, and which she knew how much he loved. They had not been able to find him, but she was going to find him soon. She swore that she was.

And so when some of them left her she remained with only a few of the tribe, with just one little wagon dragged by two starved horses and she traced her way back to the Volga, and crossed on the other side.

Like a trained hunter's dog, abandoning all her veneer of culture and relying entirely on her tracking instinct, with her nose to the ground trying to smell out my traces, she traveled on. She hardly left a man or a woman passing without inquiring about Ivan. She inquired among the Volga boatmen that she met pulling the boats. She cajoled, she told fortunes, she flattered, she sat at campfires of boatmen at night, talking to them, singing and dancing before them to get into their good graces and obtain their friendship.

Had they not seen Ivan? They all must know Ivan.

And she gave them a description of him. And some, just to win her favors, because she was so very charming, told her that he was up the river, that he had seen him at Nijni Novgorod pulling up a boat of lumber. Others told her that he was seen coming down the river. But she doubted them. She knew they were lying to her because she was almost certain Ivan was not pulling a boat just then. She figured out that he would be afraid to get back again to his old occupation, lest he be caught by the bolsheviki, to whom he had been denounced as a traitor and who were still looking for him, since she and Stephan had created such a hullabaloo about his dangerous existence.

Week after week she kept on tracking Ivan. In villages, in towns and hamlets, in inns and in camps. Finally she landed, late that fall, at Jaroslav. Something told her that he was there. Something told her that if he was not there at that moment he should arrive there. She and the other few of the tribe camped just outside of the town. Early every morning they would abandon their camp in charge of a very old gypsy woman, who was of no great use to them except for taking care of the camp, and four of them would spread out into different parts of the city, canvassing house after house, combing every nook and corner, looking into everybody's face.

Mariusha returned from the expeditions only very late at night. And although she herself was unsuccessful, when she listened to the unsuccessful reports of the others she became furious, accusing them of betraying her and of not being vigilant enough, that they cared more for the few worthless paper rubles they were trying to obtain from people than to help her get her revenge. And she had made them rich; rich beyond their dreams.

And in the morning, after a few hours' rest, she would be the first one to urge them up and out. She had so exaggerated the wrong that Ivan had done her that she had worked herself up into a passion. Even to her Ivan's existence seemed to be the greatest menace. As if the world could not be at peace unless he was destroyed and eliminated from it.

And yet it had not occurred to her to look for him in the "Americansky House."

* * * * *

The Americans returned one day bringing with them what they thought was an almost frozen gypsy woman but which Ivan immediately recognized as Vera. They stood aside and wondered open-mouthed at their tight embrace, and how they leaned heads against shoulders and wept longly without being able to let go of one another.

There were no words between the two. Their emotions were too great for words or explanations. Looking into her face, Ivan knew vaguely all that she had gone through, knew all that had happened to her soul. He knew that if his friends had found her frozen on the way, and from the manner in which she was dressed, that she had been looking for him, and that she responded to what he felt for her. He knew that in running away from the other side she had chiefly wanted to come to him. That between them was an indestructible bond which neither time nor opinion nor birth nor heredity could destroy. What good were words then!

After many hours that seemed only minutes, during which they merely pronounced one another's names as they touched one another's hands, Mr. G——, the head of the Americansky House, came in to ask Ivan:

"Now, who is this woman?"

"Why," he answered, looking at Vera, who had risen to her feet, "it is—"

"I am his wife," Vera answered simply, with great dignity, completing the answer.

"What an extraordinary thing to have found her as our men have found her," Mr. G—— mused.

"I shall explain to you all some other day," Ivan assured him, overwhelmed as he was again by Vera's answer to the question.

It eliminated in a few words all embarrassment and explained away things which he could not have known how to explain; for never would he have dared to say what she had said. Never would he have dared claim her as his wife to save explanations.

And then Mr. G—— left them again and they fell to embracing and kissing each other as if what she had said had consecrated them as man and wife.

* * * * *

The days that followed that day passed so rapidly Ivan hardly knew what was happening. They sat up whole nights and talked. He listened to her. She insisted on telling all that had happened to her, in detail, day by day. And every few minutes she would interrupt her tale and throwing her arms around Ivan and pressing him to her heart, she would cry out:

"But I was thinking of you, Ivan. All the time I was thinking of you. Even if I didn't know it I was thinking of you."

And he told her how he had lingered long in the village after she had left. And told her all that had happened. How he had been and still was tracked, as a traitor to their cause, by those who had been his friends and for whom he had suffered and worked.

It was during one of those talks that he told her what had happened between himself and Mariusha. It was only then that he explained to her Mariusha's power. And telling her the story things became much clearer. Ivan wondered whether, now that Stephan's power had been taken away from him, Mariusha had resigned herself and was living quietly with him in Moscow waiting for the tribunal either to censure or dimiss her husband!

He had caught sight of the backs of gypsies many a time during the last few days, but did not dare to go near enough to see their faces lest they recognize him. He had noticed that most of them had already disappeared when Stephan's downfall had been announced, and knew that there was a strong relation between their disappearance and the commissar's dismissal.

It had been no secret to Ivan what they had been doing. It was spoken of quite openly by many of the friends of the bolsheviki and dismissed as unimportant while the big struggle was still going on. All minor details had to be left pending until the situation was clear. There is an old Russian proverb:

"In a fire one does not save the mirror first, but the bedding."

A few days later Ivan heard about the gypsy camp outside of Jaroslav quite by accident from one of the American men. He came and sat down near Ivan and told him all about them. From his description Ivan was almost certain that it was Mariusha and a few of her tribe. But the fool who thought he had gotten so much information from them had not realized that he had given much more information in exchange. Mariusha had read his fortune. In a spirit of fun he had permitted her to do so. While she was reading his hand she was putting questions to him as to how many people there were in the Americansky House, and who they were. She explained to him that her ability to tell his good fortune depended largely on his description of the people he was with just then.

There were only two Russians in the Americansky House. One was the official interpreter. Ivan was the other one. It had been tacitly agreed between the rest of the people, because of Mr. G——'s friendship to Ivan never to speak of him to others. But that

American youngster who had learned Russian and spoke it quite fluently did not think it important to hide his identity from the gypsy woman who was telling him his fortune. He gave her only too detailed a description of Ivan.

CHAPTER XIX

IVAN told Vera about the gypsies outside the town, but not caring to alarm her he did not tell her that he thought Mariusha was in that camp. He knew also from the manner the gypsies had first enticed Vera to come with them and then abandoned her outside the town that the gypsies were closing in, but he did not want to alarm Vera.

Ivan went out of his room that night for a few moments, because he thought he had heard some noise outside his door. He remembered a sinking feeling in his eyes. A hole had opened under his feet and he was falling down. And then everything went black before him.

When he awoke from the stupor he was tied like a sausage, a bundle. He was gagged and was lying on the ground under a tent while two glistening eyes were bending over him. He had one look and closed his eyes again, expecting death, expecting at the next moment the impact of a dagger in his heart. And when it did not come he opened his eyes

A Cecil B. De Mille Production. *The Volga Boatman.*
THE ARISTOCRATS ARE FORCED TO THE HARNESS OF THE VOLGA BOAT, WHILE THE PROLETARIAT LASH THEM ON WITH BITTER TAUNTS.

again and looked at her. She took the gag out of his mouth. When he caught his breath he told her:

"Whatever it is make short work. Plunge your dagger and be done with it."

But she laughed.

"It is more than a year since I have been running after you. And do you want me to end it all in one second? Fool. Fool. You thought you could hide from me. You thought you could betray me without being punished for it. You thought you could play with a little gypsy girl and then leave her whenever you felt like it. And now that I have you in my power do you expect me to finish it all with one blow? Ah, no, Ivan. There will be plenty of time for that. Nobody will comb Russia as I have combed it to find you."

And she sat over Ivan gloating, grinning. From time to time another member of the tribe would come in to look. She would point to Ivan and they would grin and they would laugh, gloating over "their" victim, amused themselves as if he were a garroted pig they were soon going to slay for their food.

Thus passed the rest of the night.

Early at dawn the five of them held council. They spoke a more secret language than he had ever heard them speak. There was one black bearded devil amongst them who urged her to do away with Ivan immediately before it was too late. And when Mariusha argued against it he became so furious he grabbed the butt of his pistol while turning sideways toward Ivan to finish him off himself. Mariusha jumped at him and the two had a fist fight in which the others joined.

And then they quieted down after long palavers and began to talk. Mariusha talked long and passionately in a singsong voice, as if reciting some religious canto. She was telling them all that she had suffered because of him, and all that she had done for her tribe for the privilege of having Ivan in her hands to do with as she pleased when she pleased.

They were all weeping loudly when she ended her peroration. Before the sun was up Ivan was tied down, garroted as he was, to a wide board which was swung on two loops under the wagon. And they were driving on again after abandoning camp.

The pains and the torture he underwent while lying stretched out on that board and hanging from the cavorting, jerking carriage over the bad roads and into devious paths were

THE VOLGA BOATMAN

indescribable. Every time the wagon went up or down his head was thrown against the wooden floor of the wagon. He was bruised and bleeding, and numb of cold and pain. In his few moments of consciousness he hoped that the end would come, certain that he should die within the next few moments, before Mariusha should have had her revenge by her own hand.

* * * * *

When Ivan had not returned to his room after a few minutes' absence, during which Vera had sat up in bed to wait for him, though she had not heard the noise of the blow that knocked him down she became much alarmed. Without losing much time she woke up the rest of the house in which the Americanskies slept. It just so happened that the interpreter had left that night on a spree together with the young man whose knowledge of Russian had brought the whole thing on Ivan's head. After Vera had made several attempts in Russian to explain what she thought had happened, without much success, she finally resorted to her French, which the leader of the Americanskies understood. He was struck speechless to hear from this supposedly peasant woman such pure French as she spoke.

They were bewildered for a few moments, and then Vera remembered that Ivan had told her about the gypsy camp outside of Jaroslav and of Mariusha's oath and how they had been searching for him all over the country for months and months. And her intelligence told her the gypsy camp was the place to look for Ivan.

It took time before they could find horses and a sleigh to ride out of the city. And it took still more time to get outside of Jaroslav and to find the spot where the gypsy camp had been. Ivan had omitted to tell Vera in what direction from the city the gypsies were camping. But at dawn the searching party discovered where the tzigan camp had been. Nothing but the cinders of dying embers and the rut of wheels indicated where the gypsies had tented last. But a freshly falling snow soon obliterated all possible signs on the road.

After they had been searching for hours in vain over a vast area where the snow continued to fall the Americanskies, discouraged and cold, decided to give up the chase. Yet as Vera refused to leave the spot and continued to advance in the face of the snow that kept on falling thicker and thicker, they had to stand by. They could not leave a woman

THE VOLGA BOATMAN

alone in a blinding snow at dawn in a wilderness.

Something urged Vera to keep her eyes close to the ground as she advanced, zigzagging this way and that.

After they had driven on and searched for several hours the snow ceased to fall. And though there were no fresh ruts to be observed, Vera suddenly discovered glittering red spots. They were the drops of blood that had been falling off Ivan's face and his forehead as he was bumped against the bottom of the cart under which he was slung.

She was immediately certain it was his blood. Another hundred feet and again a few red spots in the snow. And then they disappeared and there was no other trace.

But Vera knew from the direction of the blood that it was the direction in which the gypsies had gone.

On and on the Americans drove. Soon they came upon fresh ruts that led to a narrow path that went through a clump of denuded trees. On they drove at a rapid pace now, encouraged by what they had discovered. And when they had come out from the clump of trees they saw the gypsy wagon at a distance riding at top speed.

At the call of the Americans to the gypsies that they stop they were answered with several shots from a gun. The Americans as well as Vera were unarmed, but they rode at top speed, and were soon within hailing distance of the gypsies, to whom they called to stop.

Either because they were afraid of the pursuing party or because they had already wasted their meager ammunition the gypsies stopped. While the others jumped off the rear of the wagon and made away in the distance Mariusha confronted the whole American party.

"What is it you want and why have you been pursuing us?" she asked with effrontery.

The Americans were trying to answer her, but Vera had immediately jumped down from the sleigh, and a single glance at Mariusha convinced her that she was the woman Ivan had described to her. Like a fury she threw herself upon the gypsy girl, with hands at her throat, yelling at her:

"You have Ivan! Give me Ivan!"

"I don't know what you are talking about," Mariusha answered, spreading her hands and showing the wagon. "Look for him if he is there."

Still holding on to the gypsy woman with

THE VOLGA BOATMAN

one hand and dragging her after her, Vera jumped into the canvas-covered cart and turned everything over while the Americans looked on. Mariusha's eyes were triumphant when Vera had climbed down from the car without finding her man.

She made a sign to the Americans that Vera was probably out of her mind, and got ready to climb back on her seat and drive away. But Vera would not let her. Holding her by the shoulders, she kept on shaking her and yelling at her that she tell her where Ivan was.

* * * * *

Ivan had been numb and had fainted repeatedly as he was lying under the wagon, bruised and broken. As if in a dream he suddenly heard Vera's voice. His mind cleared at its sound. He began to hear distinctly the end of the quarrel, Vera's cries inquiring about him, and the gypsy girl's answer.

"You have looked for him, haven't you, everywhere? What else do you want of me? I haven't eaten him. I do not know anything about him."

Ivan was gagged. He wanted to cry out to tell Vera where he was. It seemed for a moment that all was lost. The wagon would be driven on without Vera knowing how near she had been to him. And then in a supreme effort he groaned as loud as he could. And he groaned again.

There was silence after his groan. All his faculties were sharpened to note the effect of his effort. Had they heard it? Would she hear it?

"From where does that groan come?" Ivan heard Vera cry out. She jumped back into the gypsy wagon.

He groaned again.

Like a serpent gliding out from a hand that holds it, Mariusha freed herself from the circle of men that had suddenly surrounded her at the sound of that groan, and with a lurch she had thrown herself under the wagon. Ivan felt a sharp pain that went through his side.

In an instant Vera had thrown herself upon Mariusha, and flattened her out in the snow under the wagon, holding her down while Mariusha was struggling to turn over on one side to reach Ivan again with the dagger she had taken out from her hair in which it had been stuck till then. Another instant and the Americans, having finally realized what was taking place, turned over the gypsy wagon on its side. And there was Ivan.

THE VOLGA BOATMAN 231

While the men were busy cutting the ropes that held him fast the two women were fighting in the snow. And then everything went black before Ivan.

There was a woman stretched out dead in the snow with her hands wide apart, still holding the shiny blade between her clutched fingers. Vera was standing over Ivan with her hair hanging over her blood-smeared face. She took his limp hand into hers, for he had not yet recovered the use of his body, and said:

"We are quits now, Ivan, as far as one thing is concerned. You have saved my life once. I have now saved yours."

* * * * *

And then things went on very rapidly. For a good many reasons Ivan's American friends decided that he had better leave Russia at once. As the matter stood it would implicate them without in any way helping him, and probably also endanger the life of Vera.

He was too sick and too weak to oppose himself to their plans. They practically decided by themselves what to do with him. He had no voice in the matter at all. A few days later he was smuggled over the border into Finland; not before a last handshake and a last look into Vera's eyes. They did not know whether they should succeed in communicating with one another again. They did not know how they should ever meet one another again.

It took Ivan two years to reach New York. And from there he began to send letters and inquiries, and went to the general office of the Y. M. C. A. there, thinking that maybe they could give him information about the group that had been at such and such a time in Jaroslav. But the information he received was of no use. The names did not correspond with the names of his friends. He asked them to write and inquire. He waited week after week, working meanwhile at what he could get to keep body and soul together.

He was living in the lower part of New York, in one of the large tenement houses near the East River. He had made few acquaintances and did not care to make more. It was a Saturday afternoon. Ivan was getting ready to visit the office and inquire, when he heard his song, the Volga boatmen song, being played on a street organ below. He had not heard the song since he had left Russia, since he had sung it himself. He raised the window and stuck his head out with his hands full of coins from his pockets, ready to throw everything to the organ grinder below.

At that very moment another window went up, just opposite his, across the street. At the same moment coins dropped from the opposite windows in the street, dropped from the outstretched hands of two exiles suddenly meeting. There were two cries uttered at the same time. It was Vera. And she had been living there, across from Ivan's window, within hailing distance of him, three months without his knowing it.

THE END

*"The Books You Like to Read
at the Price You Like to Pay"*

There Are Two Sides to Everything—

—including the wrapper which covers every Grosset & Dunlap book. When you feel in the mood for a good romance, refer to the carefully selected list of modern fiction comprising most of the successes by prominent writers of the day which is printed on the back of every Grosset & Dunlap book wrapper.

You will find more than five hundred titles to choose from—books for every mood and every taste and every pocketbook.

Don't forget the other side, but in case the wrapper is lost, write to the publishers for a complete catalog.

*There is a Grosset & Dunlap Book
for every mood and for every taste*

EMERSON HOUGH'S NOVELS

May be had wherever books are sold. Ask for Grosset and Dunlap's list

THE COVERED WAGON

NORTH OF 36

THE WAY OF A MAN

THE STORY OF THE OUTLAW

THE SAGEBRUSHER

THE GIRL AT THE HALFWAY HOUSE

THE WAY OUT

THE MAN NEXT DOOR

THE MAGNIFICENT ADVENTURE

THE BROKEN GATE

THE STORY OF THE COWBOY

THE WAY TO THE WEST

54-40 OR FIGHT

HEART'S DESIRE

THE MISSISSIPPI BUBBLE

THE PURCHASE PRICE

GROSSET & DUNLAP, Publishers, NEW YORK

GEORGE W. OGDEN'S WESTERN NOVELS

May be had wherever books are sold. Ask for Grosset & Dunlap's list.

THE BARON OF DIAMOND TAIL
The Elk Mountain Cattle Co. had not paid a dividend in years; so Edgar Barrett, fresh from the navy, was sent West to see what was wrong at the ranch. The tale of this tenderfoot outwitting the buckaroos at their own play will sweep you into the action of this salient western novel.

THE BONDBOY
Joe Newbolt, bound out by force of family conditions to work for a number of years, is accused of murder and circumstances are against him. His mouth is sealed; he cannot, as a gentleman, utter the words that would clear him. A dramatic, romantic tale of intense interest.

CLAIM NUMBER ONE
Dr. Warren Slavens drew claim number one, which entitled him to first choice of rich lands on an Indian reservation in Wyoming. It meant a fortune; but before he established his ownership he had a hard battle with crooks and politicians.

THE DUKE OF CHIMNEY BUTTE
When Jerry Lambert, "the Duke," attempts to safeguard the cattle ranch of Vesta Philbrook from thieving neighbors, his work is appallingly handicapped because of Grace Kerr, one of the chief agitators, and a deadly enemy of Vesta's. A stirring tale of brave deeds, gun-play and a love that shines above all.

THE FLOCKMASTER OF POISON CREEK
John Mackenzie trod the trail from Jasper to the great sheep country where fortunes were being made by the flock-masters. Shepherding was not a peaceful pursuit in those bygone days. Adventure met him at every turn—there is a girl of course—men fight their best fights for a woman—it is an epic of the sheeplands.

THE LAND OF LAST CHANCE
Jim Timberlake and Capt. David Scott waited with restless thousands on the Oklahoma line for the signal to dash across the border. How the city of Victory arose overnight on the plains, how people savagely defended their claims against the "sooners;" how good men and bad played politics, makes a strong story of growth and American initiative.

TRAIL'S END
Ascalon was the end of the trail for thirsty cowboys who gave vent to their pent-up feelings without restraint. Calvin Morgan was not concerned with its wickedness until Seth Craddock's malevolence directed itself against him. He did not emerge from the maelstrom until he had obliterated every vestige of lawlessness, and assured himself of the safety of a certain dark-eyed girl.

Ask for Complete free list of G. & D. Popular Copyrighted Fiction

GROSSET & DUNLAP, Publishers, **NEW YORK**

CHARLES ALDEN SELTZER'S WESTERN NOVELS

May be had wherever books are sold. Ask for Grosset and Dunlap's list.

THE WAY OF THE BUFFALO
Jim Cameron builds a railroad adjacent to Ballantine's property, even though Ballantine threatens to kill him the day he runs it.

BRASS COMMANDMENTS
Stephen Lannon writes six commandments over six loaded cartridges set out where the evil men who threaten him and the girl he loves, may see them.

WEST!
When Josephine Hamilton went West to visit Betty, she met "Satan" Lattimer, ruthless, handsome, fascinating, who taught her some things.

SQUARE DEAL SANDERSON
Square Deal Sanderson rode onto the Double A just as an innocent man was about to be hanged and Mary Bransford was in danger of losing her property.

"BEAU" RAND
Bristling with quick, decisive action, and absorbing in its love theme, "Beau" Rand, mirrors the West of the hold-up days in remarkable fashion.

THE BOSS OF THE LAZY Y
Calumet Marston, daredevil, returns to his father's ranch to find it is being run by a young woman who remains in charge until he accepts sundry conditions.

"DRAG" HARLAN
Harlan establishes himself as the protector of Barbara Morgan and deals out punishment to the girl's enemies through the lightning flash of drawn guns.

THE TRAIL HORDE
How Kane Lawler fought the powerful interests that were trying to crush him and Ruth Hamlin, the woman he loved, makes intensely interesting reading.

THE RANCHMAN
The story of a two-fisted product of the west, pitted against a rascally spoilsman, who sought to get control of Marion Harlan and her ranch.

"FIREBRAND" TREVISON
The encroachment of the railroad brought Rosalind Benham—and also results in a clash between Corrigan and "Firebrand" that ends when the better man wins.

THE RANGE BOSS
Ruth Harkness comes West to the ranch her uncle left her. Rex Randerson, her range boss, rescues her from a mired buckboard, and is in love with her from that moment on.

THE VENGEANCE OF JEFFERSON GAWNE
A story of the Southwest that tells how the law came to a cow-town, dominated by a cattle thief. There is a wonderful girl too, who wins the love of Jefferson Gawne.

GROSSET & DUNLAP, PUBLISHERS, NEW YORK

THE NOVELS OF TEMPLE BAILEY

May be had wherever books are sold. Ask for Grosset & Dunlap's list.

"Although my ancestry is all of New England, I was born in the old town of Petersburg, Virginia. I went later to Richmond and finally at the age of five to Washington, D. C., returning to Richmond for a few years in a girl's school, which was picturesquely quartered in General Lee's mansion.

PEACOCK FEATHERS

The eternal conflict between wealth and love. Jerry, the idealist who is poor, loves Mimi, a beautiful, spoiled society girl.

THE DIM LANTERN

The romance of little Jane Barnes who is loved by two men.

THE GAY COCKADE

Unusual short stories where Miss Bailey shows her keen knowledge of character and environment, and how romance comes to different people.

THE TRUMPETER SWAN

Randy Paine comes back from France to the monotony of every-day affairs. But the girl he loves shows him the beauty in the common-place

THE TIN SOLDIER

A man who wishes to serve his country, but is bound by a tie he cannot in honor break—that's Derry. A girl who loves him, shares his humiliation and helps him to win—that's Jean. Their love is the story.

MISTRESS ANNE

A girl in Maryland teaches school, and believes that work is worthy service. Two men come to the little community; one is weak, the other strong, and both need Anne.

CONTRARY MARY

An old-fashioned love story that is nevertheless modern.

GLORY OF YOUTH

A novel that deals with a question, old and yet ever new—how far should an engagement of marriage bind two persons who discover they no longer love.

GROSSET & DUNLAP, PUBLISHERS, NEW YORK

MARGARET PEDLER'S NOVELS

May be had wherever books are sold. Ask for Grosset & Dunlap's list.

RED ASHES
A gripping story of a doctor who failed in a crucial operation—and had only himself to blame. Could the woman he loved forgive him?

THE BARBARIAN LOVER
A love story based on the creed that the only important things between birth and death are the courage to face life and the love to sweeten it.

THE MOON OUT OF REACH
Nan Davenant's problem is one that many a girl has faced—her own happiness or her father's bond.

THE HOUSE OF DREAMS-COME-TRUE
How a man and a woman fulfilled a gypsy's strange prophecy.

THE HERMIT OF FAR END
How love made its way into a walled-in house and a walled-in heart.

THE LAMP OF FATE
The story of a woman who tried to take all and give nothing.

THE SPLENDID FOLLY
Do you believe that husbands and wives should have no secrets from each other?

THE VISION OF DESIRE
An absorbing romance written with all that sense of feminine tenderness that has given the novels of Margaret Pedler their universal appeal.

GROSSET & DUNLAP, Publishers, NEW YORK

RUBY M. AYRES' NOVELS

May be had wherever books are sold. Ask for Grosset & Dunlap's list

THE LITTL'ST LOVER

CANDLE LIGHT

THE MAN WITHOUT A HEART

THE ROMANCE OF A ROGUE

THE MATHERSON MARRIAGE

RICHARD CHATTERTON

A BACHELOR HUSBAND

THE SCAR

THE MARRIAGE OF BARRY WICKLOW

THE UPHILL ROAD

WINDS OF THE WORLD

THE SECOND HONEYMOON

THE PHANTOM LOVER

GROSSET & DUNLAP, Publishers, NEW YORK

PETER B. KYNE'S NOVELS

May be had wherever books are sold.   Ask for Grosset and Dunlap's list.

THE ENCHANTED HILL
A gorgeous story with a thrilling mystery and a beautiful girl.

NEVER THE TWAIN SHALL MEET
A romance of California and the South Seas.

CAPPY RICKS RETIRES
Cappy retires, but the romance of the sea and business, keep calling him back, and he comes back strong.

THE PRIDE OF PALOMAR
When two strong men clash and the under-dog has Irish blood in his veins—there's a tale that Kyne can tell!

KINDRED OF THE DUST
Donald McKay, son of Hector McKay, millionaire lumber king, falls in love with "Nan of the sawdust pile," a charming girl who has been ostracized by her townsfolk.

THE VALLEY OF THE GIANTS
The fight of the Cardigans, father and son, to hold the Valley of the Giants against treachery.

CAPPY RICKS
Cappy Ricks gave Matt Peasley the acid test because he knew it was good for his soul.

WEBSTER: MAN'S MAN
A man and a woman hailing from the "States," met up with a revolution while in Central America. Adventures and excitement came so thick and fast that their love affair had to wait for a lull in the game.

CAPTAIN SCRAGGS
This sea yarn recounts the adventures of three rapscallion seafaring men.

THE LONG CHANCE
Harley P. Hennage is the best gambler, the best and worst man of San Pasqual and of lovely Donna.

GROSSET & DUNLAP, Publishers, NEW YORK

JACKSON GREGORY'S NOVELS

May be had wherever books are sold. Ask for Grosset and Dunlap's list.

DAUGHTER OF THE SUN

A tale of Aztec treasure—of American adventurers, who seek it—of Zoraida, who hides it.

TIMBER-WOLF

This is a story of action and of the wide open, dominated always by the heroic figure of Timber-Wolf.

THE EVERLASTING WHISPER

The story of a strong man's struggle against savage nature and humanity, and of a beautiful girl's regeneration from a spoiled child of wealth into a courageous strong-willed woman.

DESERT VALLEY

A college professor sets out with his daughter to find gold. They meet a rancher who loses his heart, and becomes involved in a feud.

MAN TO MAN

How Steve won his game and the girl he loved, is a story filled with breathless situations.

THE BELLS OF SAN JUAN

Dr. Virginia Page is forced to go with the sheriff on a night journey into the strongholds of a lawless band.

JUDITH OF BLUE LAKE RANCH

Judith Sanford part owner of a cattle ranch realizes she is being robbed by her foreman. With the help of Bud Lee, she checkmates Trevor's scheme.

THE SHORT CUT

Wayne is suspected of killing his brother after a quarrel. Financial complications, a horse-race and beautiful Wanda, make up a thrilling romance.

THE JOYOUS TROUBLE MAKER

A reporter sets up housekeeping close to Beatrice's Ranch much to her chagrin. There is "another man" who complicates matters.

SIX FEET FOUR

Beatrice Waverly is robbed of $5,000 and suspicion fastens upon Buck Thornton, but she soon realizes he is not guilty.

WOLF BREED

No Luck Drennan, a woman hater and sharp of tongue, finds a match in Ygerne whose clever fencing wins the admiration and love of the "Lone Wolf."

GROSSET & DUNLAP,   PUBLISHERS,   NEW YORK

THE NOVELS OF
GRACE LIVINGSTON HILL
(MRS. LUTZ)

May be had wherever books are sold.   Ask for Grosset & Dunlap's list

BEST MAN, THE
CITY OF FIRE, THE
CLOUDY JEWEL
DAWN OF THE MORNING
ENCHANTED BARN, THE
EXIT BETTY
FINDING OF JASPER HOLT, THE
GIRL FROM MONTANA, THE
LO, MICHAEL!
MAN OF THE DESERT, THE
MARCIA SCHUYLER
MIRANDA
MYSTERY OF MARY, THE
OBSESSION OF VICTORIA GRACEN, THE
PHOEBE DEANE
RED SIGNAL, THE
SEARCH, THE
STORY OF A WHIM, THE
TOMORROW ABOUT THIS TIME
TRYST, THE
VOICE IN THE WILDERNESS, A
WITNESS, THE

Ask for Complete free list of G. & D. Popular Copyrighted Fiction

GROSSET & DUNLAP, Publishers, **NEW YORK**

JAMES OLIVER CURWOOD'S
STORIES OF ADVENTURE

May be had wherever books are sold. Ask for Grosset & Dunlap's list.

THE COUNTRY BEYOND

THE FLAMING FOREST

THE VALLEY OF SILENT MEN

THE RIVER'S END

THE GOLDEN SNARE

NOMADS OF THE NORTH

KAZAN

BAREE, SON OF KAZAN

THE COURAGE OF CAPTAIN PLUM

THE DANGER TRAIL

THE HUNTED WOMAN

THE FLOWER OF THE NORTH

THE GRIZZLY KING

ISOBEL

THE WOLF HUNTERS

THE GOLD HUNTERS

THE COURAGE OF MARGE O'DOONE

BACK TO GOD'S COUNTRY

Ask for Complete free list of G. & D. Popular Copyrighted Fiction

GROSSET & DUNLAP, PUBLISHERS, NEW YORK

ZANE GREY'S NOVELS

May be had wherever books are sold. Ask for Grosset and Dunlap's list.

- THE CALL OF THE CANYON
- WANDERER OF THE WASTELAND
- TO THE LAST MAN
- THE MYSTERIOUS RIDER
- THE MAN OF THE FOREST
- THE DESERT OF WHEAT
- THE U. P. TRAIL
- WILDFIRE
- THE BORDER LEGION
- THE RAINBOW TRAIL
- THE HERITAGE OF THE DESERT
- RIDERS OF THE PURPLE SAGE
- THE LIGHT OF WESTERN STARS
- THE LAST OF THE PLAINSMEN
- THE LONE STAR RANGER
- DESERT GOLD
- BETTY ZANE
- THE DAY OF THE BEAST

* * * * * * *

LAST OF THE GREAT SCOUTS

The life story of "Buffalo Bill" by his sister Helen Cody Wetmore, with Foreword and conclusion by Zane Grey.

ZANE GREY'S BOOKS FOR BOYS

- KEN WARD IN THE JUNGLE
- THE YOUNG LION HUNTER
- THE YOUNG FORESTER
- THE YOUNG PITCHER
- THE SHORT STOP
- THE RED-HEADED OUTFIELD AND OTHER BASEBALL STORIES

GROSSET & DUNLAP, Publishers, NEW YORK

"STORM COUNTRY" BOOKS BY
GRACE MILLER WHITE

May be had wherever books are sold. Ask for Grosset & Dunlap's list.

JUDY OF ROGUES' HARBOR

Judy's untutored ideas of God, her love of wild things, her faith in life are quite as inspiring as those of Tess. Her faith and sincerity catch at your heart strings. This book has all of the mystery and tense action of the other Storm Country books.

TESS OF THE STORM COUNTRY

It was as Tess, beautiful, wild, impetuous, that Mary Pickford made her reputation as a motion picture actress. How love acts upon a temperament such as hers—a temperament that makes a woman an angel or an outcast, according to the character of the man she loves—is the theme of the story.

THE SECRET OF THE STORM COUNTRY

The sequel to "Tess of the Storm Country," with the same wild background, with its half-gypsy life of the squatters—tempestuous, passionate, brooding. Tess learns the "secret" of her birth and finds happiness and love through her boundless faith in life.

FROM THE VALLEY OF THE MISSING

A haunting story with its scene laid near the country familiar to readers of "Tess of the Storm Country."

ROSE O' PARADISE

"Jinny" Singleton, wild, lovely, lonely, but with a passionate yearning for music, grows up in the house of Lafe Grandoken, a crippled cobbler of the Storm Country. Her romance is full of power and glory and tenderness.

Ask for Complete free list of G. & D. Popular Copyrighted Fiction

GROSSET & DUNLAP, PUBLISHERS, NEW YORK